The

The Earl laughed and said:

"You need not worry about me, Valencia. There are no more gentlemen with revolvers hiding in the umbrella-stand, and I promise you I am very careful about what I eat and drink."

Valencia drew in her breath before she said:

"You are making a joke of it, but I cannot help feeling that you are not yet out . . . of reach of those people!"

"Valencia," the Earl said, "I want you to enjoy yourself here in London, and to think only of yourself."

But as Valencia looked at the Earl she fancied that just behind him like a shadow was Lady Hester Stansfield, watching and waiting, like a tigress, determined sooner or later to spring on her prey.

It was then, as a steel of fear flashed through her heart, that Valencia knew she loved him . . .

A Camfield Novel of Love
by Barbara Cartland

"Barbara Cartland's novels are all distinguished by their intelligence, good sense, and good nature . . ."
— **ROMANTIC TIMES**

"Who could give better advice on how to keep your romance going strong than the world's most famous romance novelist, Barbara Cartland?"
— **THE STAR**

Camfield Place,
Hatfield
Hertfordshire,
England

Dearest Reader,

Camfield Novels of Love mark a very exciting era of my books with Jove. They have already published nearly two hundred of my titles since they became my first publisher in America, and now all my original paperback romances in the future will be published exclusively by them.

As you already know, Camfield Place in Hertfordshire is my home, which originally existed in 1275, but was rebuilt in 1867 by the grandfather of Beatrix Potter.

It was here in this lovely house, with the best view in the county, that she wrote *The Tale of Peter Rabbit*. Mr. McGregor's garden is exactly as she described it. The door in the wall that the fat little rabbit could not squeeze underneath and the goldfish pool where the white cat sat twitching its tail are still there.

I had Camfield Place blessed when I came here in 1950 and was so happy with my husband until he died, and now with my children and grandchildren, that I know the atmosphere is filled with love and we have all been very lucky.

It is easy here to write of love and I know you will enjoy the Camfield Novels of Love. Their plots are definitely exciting and the covers very romantic. They come to you, like all my books, with love.

Bless you,

A NEW CAMFIELD NOVEL OF LOVE BY

BARBARA CARTLAND

The Earl Escapes

JOVE BOOKS, NEW YORK

THE EARL ESCAPES

A Jove Book / published by arrangement with
the author

PRINTING HISTORY
Jove edition / September 1987

ISBN: 0-515-09167-7

Jove Books are published by The Berkley Publishing Group,
200 Madison Avenue, New York, New York 10016.
The name "JOVE" and the "J" logo
are trademarks belonging to Jove Publications, Inc.

PRINTED IN THE UNITED STATES OF AMERICA

10 9 8 7 6 5 4 3 2 1

Author's Note

BECAUSE the Catholic Church would not agree to King Henry VIII divorcing one wife to marry another, there followed the period known as the Dissolution of the Monasteries, when Catholic Churches and buildings were wrecked and Priests went in fear of their lives.

It was at this time that Priests' Holes were built into Churches and Stately Homes owned by Catholics in order to save their Priests from being slaughtered.

These consisted of tiny rooms no bigger than cupboards, where a Priest could have a small altar, a crucifix, and a chair, and here he would wait until the danger was passed.

There were many ingenious ways of concealing Priests' Holes. One could lift the tread of a stair like the lid of a box and inside find a staircase leading down to a cellar where a Priest could hide.

The Priests' Hole I describe in this novel resembles the one in Madresfield Court in Worcestershire, for many years the family seat of the Earls Beauchamp.

chapter one

1886

VALENCIA Hadley arranged the flowers she had brought in from the garden in an attractive Chinese vase.

She thought as she did so that it would be surprising if the Earl was impressed by them.

Anyway, the house looked more lived in than it would without flowers.

It always hurt her that the ancient rooms, with their tapestries, their embroidered curtains, and their antique furniture, looked dull and empty.

It was as if they needed people to restore them to the life they had originally known at Dolphin Priory.

That meant that some of the chests, pictures, and carpets were at least three centuries old.

It was, therefore, not surprising that they appeared a little dulled with age.

At the same time, she loved the house and everything in it.

It had always been, in a way, her home.

She spent many hours arranging the flowers in the long Drawing-Room whose windows looked out on the Rose Garden.

She also put them in the hall with its dark panelling and its tattered flags.

These were relics of the many battles in which the Earl's ancestors had participated.

"Does it not seem strange, Papa," she had said a week ago, "that the Earl has now been back in England for six months, yet he has not paid us a visit?"

"I expect, my dear," her father replied, "that after so many years abroad, he is enjoying himself among the bright lights of London, and has no wish to bury himself in the country."

Valencia was just about to say that she did not feel in the least "buried."

Then she realised her father was teasing her, as he often did, about her preoccupation with Dolphin Priory.

The Sixth Earl of Dolphinston had inherited quite unexpectedly after his cousins had been killed.

One in the siege of Khartoum and the other in India.

It had been a bitter blow for their father.

After the death of his younger son, William, he had given up any interest in living and had died slowly from, Valencia believed, a broken heart.

Valencia's mother, who had died several years earlier, had been a second cousin of the late Earl, and her father was his private Chaplain.

It had been quite a long time before they had any news of the heir to the ancient title and the three-thousand acres in which the house stood.

He owned other properties in various parts of England.

But Dolphin Priory was the traditional seat of the Earls of Dolphinston.

It was expected by all those who worked there that their new master would be interested enough to pay them a visit as soon as he returned to England.

Although it often took a long time for news to reach them from London, they had heard that he had been an extremely brave soldier.

He had been awarded several medals for gallantry.

There had been little else known about him except that he was a cousin.

Neither he nor his father in the memory of any of those who lived on the estate had ever visited Dolphin Priory.

"You would have thought," Valencia said, following her own train of thought, "that the new Earl would at least be interested in his inheritance, and wish to see his new possessions, even if he was not particularly excited about them."

The Vicar thought the same thing, but he was too tactful to say so.

Instead, with his usual kindness of heart he found excuses for the new Earl's behaviour.

But Valencia continued to think it extraordinary.

"And now at last," she said as she stood back to appreciate her arrangement of flowers, "he is coming home."

She wondered what he would look like.

Would he have the same air of authority, the same dignity which had distinguished not only the old Earl but both of his sons?

She had not seen them very often because they had served so long overseas.

In fact, when they were killed, she had not seen George, the elder, for five years and William for seven.

She was then, of course, very young.

Yet it was not difficult to remember how handsome they were and how kind to everybody who worked for them.

These were nearly all skilled workers in occupations which had been handed down from father to son.

The estate carpenter, for instance, was the sixth generation of carpenters to work on the Dolphin Estate.

The Head Gardener had succeeded his father, his grandfather, and his great-grandfather.

The same story applied to almost everyone.

From the game-keepers who kept the woods free of vermin, even though nobody shot there anymore.

To the farmers who despite hard times had always managed to make the livestock reared at Dolphin Priory an example to the rest of the County.

Valencia looked around the Drawing-Room with its vases of lilac and syringa.

She thought that her efforts were even more attractive than usual.

"I hope His Lordship is grateful!" she said aloud with a little smile.

Then she remembered that if he did notice the

floral arrangements, he would suppose that the gardeners had done them.

He would not realise that neither Colton nor the men under him had any artistic aptitude.

They were, therefore, only too willing to leave it to her.

She went out of the Drawing-Room and saw the big bowl of tulips in the hall.

It made a striking contrast with the dark Jacobean panelling.

Then, as if she could not help it, she went into the Library to find herself some books to read.

She did so in case her father gave her instructions, which she was sure he would, that she was not to go into the house again until His Lordship had left.

"We must make sure, my dearest," her father had said only last week, "that when the new Earl does arrive, he does not think we are imposing on him."

He paused before he continued:

"It is very easy for a young man to be upset by continually being told 'That is what we have always done' or 'This is the way your predecessor behaved.' In fact, it is enough to make anyone with spirit feel rebellious!"

He had to laugh as he spoke.

Valencia thought it was so like her father to think of other people's feelings rather than his own.

At the same time, she could not help hoping that the new Earl would not introduce too many changes in the way things had always been run.

The late Earl had, with the help of his sons, made everything, she thought, as perfect as was humanly possible.

For anyone with new ideas to start changing anything in the house or in the grounds would obviously upset the old servants.

They were set in their ways.

It would especially offend them when they had thought through all the long years when there had been no mistress at Dolphin Priory, they had done their best.

'Perhaps the new Earl will get married,' Valencia thought, 'and that might prove disastrous for us all.'

She was actually thinking of herself.

She so enjoyed having what was called "the run of the house."

Ever since she had been a little girl, she had lived in the small but attractive house next to the Chapel.

It had been assigned, when the Big House was first built, to the Earl of Dolphinston's private Chaplain.

She had therefore been accepted in the Big House and granted what she knew were special privileges.

When she was a child, she had been adored by the Countess who always regretted that, despite having produced two sons, she had never had a daughter.

Valencia had also been spoilt by the Earl's servants because they loved her mother and her father.

They knew they could always turn to them with any personal problems they might have.

The Vicar was not only private Chaplain to the Earl.

He was also in charge of the small Norman Church in the village.

This was about half-a-mile down the long drive bordered by oak trees.

On Sundays there were always two Services in the village Church.

Also one in the Priory Chapel for the household.

Besides the indoor servants, there were the gardeners and grooms who lived in the cottages which were clustered round the Big House.

After the Earl became so crippled that he could never leave his rooms on the first floor, Valencia, at his request, sat in the family pew for the Services her father took in the village.

"I do not like to think of the pew being empty," the old Earl had said to Valencia, "and as you are very pretty, my dear, you will brighten it up, and I know everybody would like to see you there."

"Perhaps they will think I am . . . presuming in your . . . absence," Valencia said.

She had looked up at him anxiously.

At sixteen she had no idea that she was already outstandingly lovely, or how much the Earl appreciated her beauty.

"You do as you are told," he said gruffly, "and say a special prayer for me."

"I always do that," Valencia replied.

He had smiled and told her he was glad of her prayers.

But she thought now it would be very presumptuous to continue sitting in the family pew without being invited to do so.

Also to walk about the house as she had done for so long as if she owned it, and to borrow books without permission.

"I cannot ask him until he arrives," she placated her conscience.

She took two books down from a high shelf where she hoped they would not be missed.

They were history books which she had been meaning to read for some time.

She thought as they were heavy and closely printed they would keep her busy until she could ask the Earl if she might borrow some more.

Or when he left she could go back to the Library and help herself, as she had always done.

Then, because she knew that time was passing and the Earl might arrive from London at the station at about four o'clock, she hurried from the house.

She walked through the garden towards the door in the Elizabethan wall.

It led through an orchard into the garden of the Chaplain's House.

There was, because it had been built so long ago, an underground passage leading from the Chapel to their own house.

Over the years it had grown damp and smelt musty, so that the Vicar seldom used it.

Even Valencia, although it fascinated her, found it gloomy and rather unpleasant.

There were all sorts of "Priests' Holes" and what were called "secret passages" in the Priory which George and William had enjoyed as boys.

They had jumped out at the housemaids when they least expected it, making them scream.

They hid from their Tutors, who gave up searching for them after a while, and waited to punish them when they reappeared.

Valencia knew them all, but what she liked more than anything else was being in the gardens.

She would wander through the shrubbery and down to the lake to feed the swans and the wild duck.

They did not seem as frightened of her as they were of everyone else.

She reached the Chaplain's House, which was an enchanting example of Tudor architecture.

She found her father sitting in the low-ceilinged Study with some papers in front of him.

"Are you busy, Papa?" she asked.

"Never too busy for you, my dearest," he answered.

He glanced at the books she held under her arms and said:

"I need not ask where you have been?"

"I have borrowed something to read, Papa, because I know you are going to forbid me to go to the Big House until the Earl has left."

"You have anticipated my thoughts." The Vicar smiled. "We must not impose ourselves on the new Earl, but should leave him to find his own way about, which I am sure he will do very competently."

"How can you be sure of that?" Valencia asked just for the pleasure of arguing.

"With his brilliant command of troops the Earl has made a name for himself in the Army and has been decorated for gallantry," the Vicar replied.

He saw his daughter was listening and went on:

"He cannot, therefore, be incompetent when it comes to running an estate and I do not think he will find anything very much wrong with the Priory."

He paused.

"After all, the people who have served the Dolphinstons for so many years think of it as their own, and give themselves whole-heartedly to its welfare."

"I hope that is what you will tell the new Earl, Papa," Valencia said.

"I hear he is bringing a party down with him," the Vicar said, as if he were following his own thoughts.

"Who told you that?" Valencia enquired.

"Mr. Rawlins. He came to see me after you had left. He told me he had received a letter from His Lordship saying he was bringing a party down from London with him, and hoped that everything would be done in a satisfactory manner."

"Of course it will be!" Valencia said indignantly. "No one cooks as well as Mrs. Brooke, even though she is nearly seventy."

"I know that, my dearest," the Vicar said quietly, "but you can understand the Earl, who has never been here, being apprehensive in case his friends are uncomfortable, or the food inedible."

Valencia laughed, but she thought that the Earl had a lot to learn about his own possessions.

She only hoped he would not make trouble while he was doing so.

In the quiet of the Chaplain's House she had no idea as the evening passed what was going on at the Priory.

She was sure, however, it would not be long before somebody came to tell them every detail of what was taking place.

There was no one that night.

When she came down to breakfast and was pouring out a second cup of coffee for her father, Nanny, who had been with them for many years, came to say that Mrs. Brooke was in the kitchen and would like a word with the Vicar.

Valencia looked at her father.

"What do you think has happened?" she asked.

"That is what we are about to be told," he replied, and added, "Ask Mrs. Brooke to come in here, Nanny; I expect you have already given her a cup of tea?"

"Of course I have, Sir! And she needed it!" Nanny replied haughtily.

Now Valencia looked across the table apprehensively at her father.

"Mrs. Brooke is easily upset," he said.

There was no time to say any more, for at that moment the door opened, and Nanny announced:

"Mrs. Brooke, Sir!"

The old cook came into the room.

She was a large woman with greying hair and cheeks like rosy apples.

When she laughed it seemed to shake her whole body like blancmange.

Valencia had loved her ever since she was a child when she had made her gingerbread men for her parties.

She also always kept brandy snaps in a special tin in the kitchen for when she visited her.

Now as she dropped a small curtsy to the Vicar she said:

"It's kind o'ye to see me so early, Sir, but I 'ad to come to you!"

"Yes, of course," the Vicar said. "Sit down, Mrs. Brooke and tell me what is troubling you."

"Trouble's the right word, Sir! I don't know what

'is late Lordship, God rest his soul, would say if 'e knew what was a-goin' on!"

Valencia's eyes widened in surprise, but she did not say anything. Mrs. Brooke went on:

"What I've come to ask you, Sir, is if ye think I should engage Mary Duncan or Gladys Bell to 'elp in the kitchen. I've got to 'ave somebody—that's for sure! I can't go on as it was last night, for it's more than flesh and blood can stand!"

"Suppose you tell me from the beginning what has gone wrong?" the Vicar suggested quietly.

"It's 'is Lordship's guests, Sir. I've never 'eard nothin' like it! From the minute they comes into the 'ouse they was a-wantin' somethin'. First it was tea for the ladies and wine for the gent'men. Then it was milk for one lady—not for to drink, but for to wash her face, if you can credit it!"

She shook her head before continuing:

"After that they was orderin' *'tisanes'* just afore they went to bed, an' all this while I was a-tryin' to get dinner ready for eight, when we only expected four, an' that meant there wasn't enough trout to go round."

Mrs. Brooke paused for breath, but she was shaking from indignity.

Valencia knew how much it had all upset her.

"I am afraid, Mrs. Brooke," the Vicar said very quietly, "we live in the country and are not used to London ways. I expect all the things you mentioned are what fashionable ladies require as a matter of course."

"Well, all I can say is I wants one, if not two more girls in the kitchen, an' believe it or not, this morning the ladies is all lyin' in bed, and I've had to send their breakfasts up to them!"

Mrs. Brooke spoke as if it were something so scandalous that she could hardly speak of it.

It was with great difficulty that Valencia prevented herself from laughing.

She knew it was usual for everybody, in even the most fashionable house, to breakfast downstairs at about nine to nine-thirty. As did the Queen and the Princess of Wales.

Only if someone were ill did they expect to have breakfast taken upstairs to them.

However, there were occasions in the past when some of the Earl's more aged relatives had asked for breakfast upstairs.

This had caused quite a commotion because they had not any breakfast sets which Burrows the old Butler considered good enough to be used for the guests in question.

Only after complaints to the Earl, were two sets purchased from London to set on one side in a cupboard.

There they remained until there was a further demand for them.

Because she could not contain her curiosity, Valencia enquired:

"How many ladies breakfasted upstairs, Mrs. Brooke?"

"Three o' them, Miss," Mrs. Brooke replied. "Three! And us with only two breakfast sets, an' Mr. Burrows in a tizzy trying to arrange a third tray which never looked right, 'owever hard he tried to make it!"

"I quite understand it being a surprise to you," the Vicar said, "but I expect the ladies were tired after their journey and perhaps tomorrow things will be different."

"I very much doubt it, Sir," Mrs. Brooke said. "Already I've been told one lady will require coffee during the morning, another has a special concoction she's brought with her as has to be 'eated up, an' the third was asleep when she was called and hasn't yet given 'er orders, but doubtless I shall get them!"

She drew in her breath, then said:

"I'm too old, Vicar, and that's the truth, for this sort o' commotion! I was a-thinkin' o' retiring afore 'is Lordship came 'ome, an' now it's very much in me mind that it's somethin' I should do afore I'm run orf me feet an' in me grave even before I'm aware of it!"

"Now, you know, Mrs. Brooke," the Vicar said consolingly, "that the Priory could not do without you. I suggest, therefore, that while His Lordship is here you engage Gladys Bell, who is a very nice girl."

He stopped speaking to smile at her before he went on:

"It might be a good idea to ask her mother, who is an excellent woman, to give you a hand temporarily. I feel sure she would be only too willing to oblige."

Mrs. Brooke looked at the Vicar with an expression of satisfaction on her face.

"There now, Sir! I never thought o' that! I knowed if I came 'ere you would 'elp me an' make it right with 'is Lordship's Manager, who's always tellin' us there's too many on the pay-roll as it is. But I can't manage with the two I 'as in the kitchen at the moment, an' that's a fact!"

"I appreciate that, Mrs. Brooke," the Vicar said. "Leave it to me. I will speak to Mr. Rawlins sometime today. I am sure he will understand and knows like me that the Priory would never be the same if you left it."

"I only hopes 'is Lordship feels the same as you do, Sir," Mrs. Brooke said.

She rose with a little difficulty, as she was very fat, and said:

"I'd better be gettin' back, but I'll ask if a groom can take a message to Gladys Bell and her mother."

"Yes, do that," the Vicar said. "I've known Gladys all her life, since I christened her. She will do her best, although it is always difficult for you to teach anyone when you have so much to do."

"That's the truth—every word of it!" Mrs. Brooke said. "Thank you, Sir, thank you very much. I knowed you wouldn't let me down."

She went from the room, and as she closed the door, Valencia gave a little laugh.

"Oh, Papa, can you not imagine the commotion? The ladies asking for *tisanes*, things Mrs. Brooke has never heard of! Of course she is horrified!"

"If you ask me," the Vicar said, "she is making it sound rather worse than it really is because she has had her eye on Gladys for some time."

He sighed before he added:

"But Rawlins was firm that nobody now should be engaged at the Priory until he could talk over such matters with the Earl."

"Well, anything would be better than losing Mrs. Brooke!"

"I agree with you," the Vicar said, "and I am sure Rawlins will feel the same. At the same time, we must not forget the new Master may have ideas of his own."

"Then I only hope they are ours," Valencia said sighing.

But she felt very curious.

She knew it was a great mistake to go up to the Priory.

Yet she could not resist walking through their own orchard to where there was some high ground at the end of it.

From there she could look over the garden surrounding the house and down to the lake.

Because the sunshine was turning the water to gold and there were still some late daffodils under the trees in the Park, it looked very beautiful.

She thought that no man who had inherited anything so lovely could be anything but content.

Then, as she looked, she was aware that somebody was riding from the house over the bridge that spanned the lake.

She saw there were two men on horseback.

With a little leap of her heart she was sure one of them was the Earl.

There was something about him that reminded her of George and William.

It was perhaps the breadth of his shoulders, the way he held his head high, and the experienced manner in which he sat his horse.

"That is the Earl—I am sure of it!" she told herself.

She watched as he and the man with him reached the Park and started to move quickly beneath the trees.

Beyond the wood there was some flat ground on which they could gallop their horses.

She longed to be with them but knew that she dare not take any of the horses out of the stable without the new Earl's permission.

She had regularly ridden the horses which, because several of the grooms were growing old, needed the exercise she could give them.

The horses would be waiting for her as she entered the stable to see them in the morning.

When they nuzzled their noses against her she felt that the ones she was not riding were jealous of the one being saddled for her.

There was no need to have a groom accompany her, as would ordinarily have been correct.

She knew every inch of the land around the house and everyone in the village as well as those who worked on the estate.

They would tell her their joys and sorrows and sometimes their complaints.

She would listen to them and suggest they see her father in the evening.

Sometimes they did, but sometimes they would say:

"I feels better now I've talked to you, Miss Valencia. I just had to get it off me chest, so to speak."

"I understand," Valencia would tell them.

Then she would ride away, knowing that none of the troubles at Dolphin Priory were very big ones.

Later in the day they had a visit from the Earl's secretary, who looked after the London house.

He was a middle-aged man who had served the late Earl and was an old friend of the Vicar.

"It is lovely to see you, Mr. Stevenson," Valencia said when she found him in her father's Study.

"And you are looking prettier than ever, Miss Valencia!" he replied.

"What is happening at the Priory?" Valencia asked eagerly.

Mr. Stevenson hesitated for a moment.

Then he thought what he could say to the Vicar and Valencia might be indiscreet.

"Well, things are a little difficult because it is all new to His Lordship, and he has had a great deal to do at the War Office which has prevented him from coming to the country until now."

"So that was the reason!" Valencia exclaimed.

Mr. Stevenson nodded.

"The Secretary of State for Foreign Affairs thinks very highly of His Lordship, and although I kept asking him when he would like to come down here, it has been impossible for him to leave London."

"How will he be able to see everything if he has a party with him?" Valencia asked.

She knew as soon as she spoke that Mr. Stevenson did not wish to answer this question.

Then the Vicar, as if he also were interested, asked:

"Who are in the party, by the way? Anyone who has been here before?"

"No, no one," Mr. Stevenson replied. "But you may have heard of Lady Hester Stansfield."

"I do not think so," the Vicar answered.

"She is acclaimed as one of the most beautiful women in London," Mr. Stevenson explained, "and it is not surprising that she has a great number of admirers."

He did not sound as though he admired Lady Hester himself, and Valencia asked:

"Is she very beautiful?"

"Very!" Mr. Stevenson affirmed. "At the same time, I find Her Ladyship very difficult and very demanding."

"In what way?" the Vicar enquired.

"Well, she has made a great many changes in the London house," Mr. Stevenson said. "In fact, she behaves as if she owns it, and although it is well known that His Lordship says he has no wish to marry, I would not be surprised, Vicar, if you are not shortly asked to officiate at his wedding!"

"Goodness gracious me!" the Vicar exclaimed. "I had no idea there was anything like that in the air!"

"I do hope Lady Hester will not make a lot of changes here," Valencia said in a small voice.

"I am afraid you will have to be prepared for them, Miss Valencia," Mr. Stevenson replied. "I understand when she was married to Mr. Stansfield, who died of a heart-attack last year, she was continually redecorating and rearranging his house in Hampshire, and everybody was at odds over her demands."

Valencia gave a little cry of horror.

"But . . . she cannot alter the Priory! It is lovely as it is. All it needs is for the Earl to live here."

"If he was married and had a family, then I am sure things would be quite different," the Vicar said.

Valencia knew her father was putting the best complexion on the situation.

But she knew Mr. Stevenson too well not to realise that Lady Hester had upset him.

She could imagine nothing worse than having everything at the Priory changed.

Perhaps old servants would be replaced with new and younger ones.

Then almost like a ray of hope she said:

"Has the Earl really said he has no wish to be married?"

"It is something I have always heard talked about in London," Mr. Stevenson said, "but since his return there have been quite a number of ladies trying to persuade him differently."

"Why should he wish to remain unmarried?" the Vicar asked.

"Someone who served with him told me that he said he travelled faster without encumbrances, but I think that actually he had an unfortunate love-affair when he was a mere Subaltern, and it has put him against women."

He thought Valencia looked surprised, and he explained:

"As he is so busy, His Lordship has allowed Lady Hester to arrange parties at the house in London, and she has taken it upon herself to introduce him to the Social World."

"So it is Her Ladyship's friends who have come

with him here and who are upsetting Mrs. Brooke!" the Vicar interposed.

"Why? What on earth can she have done to Mrs. Brooke!" Mr. Stevenson exclaimed.

The Vicar explained, and Mr. Stevenson said:

"I am only thankful you have been able to arrange things so well, Vicar. I do not mind telling you, I have had great trouble with the staff in London."

He sighed before he continued:

"Her Ladyship complained about Chef after Chef whom I engaged, and found fault with other members of the household until I have not known whether I was on my head or my heels!"

"She sounds very tiresome!" Valencia thought.

But she also hoped she would have a chance to see Her Ladyship.

She knew her father would not approve if she went anywhere near the Priory without being invited.

Then she had an idea.

After Mr. Stevenson had left and the Vicar went to his Study, she went into the underground passage which led to the Chapel.

She carried with her some extra flowers which she had picked from the garden to place in the vases near the altar.

There were some already there.

But while she had arranged the flowers in the Drawing-Room and the other rooms she had neglected the Chapel simply because it was only Friday.

She always did the flowers there on Saturday so that they were fresh for the Vicar's Service on Sunday.

Now, she thought, if he found her arranging the flowers on the altar he would think only that she was making the Chapel look attractive.

He would not suspect she had any other idea in her mind.

'Perhaps,' Valencia thought, 'after I have done the flowers, I could just slip into the house, and if I went up to the third floor, and looked down into the hall, I would see Her Ladyship and some of the other members of the house-party.'

It was just a thought, and because she knew the house so well, she knew that she could see and not be seen.

No one would have the least idea that she was there.

She opened the door which led from the passage into the Vestry of the Chapel.

As she expected, because it was so seldom used, she had to push it quite hard to get it to open.

In the Vestry was her father's surplice and pile of old hymn-books.

There were also the Registers in which were noted the births, deaths, and marriages that had taken place among the family and household staff since the Chapel had first been built in 1553.

It was some time since Valencia had read them.

She thought now that if the Earl married, her father would perhaps be adding a Christening and an heir to the Earldom.

"He might have a daughter like me," Valencia told herself with a little smile, "and that would not be half so important."

She put the flowers down on a table in the Vestry

and was just going into the Chapel, when she heard somebody speak.

Instantly she stiffened and stood very still.

There were only heavy curtains over the doorway that led from the Vestry into the Chapel.

Her father had had the door removed because he said it was cumbersome, inconvenient, and invariably creaky whenever he opened it.

Now, standing still behind the curtain, Valencia was aware there were three people in the Chapel.

"We will carry him in here," the man's voice said, "and put him as near as possible to the altar. Then . . . and not before . . . I will fetch his Chaplain. I have found out where he lives."

"I suppose there will be no difficulty in getting him to perform the Marriage Service?" another man asked.

"Why should there be?" a woman's voice questioned. "After all, he is only a paid servant to His Lordship, and if he argues, you can threaten him."

"I think that would be a mistake," the first man replied, "unless it is absolutely necessary."

"What is absolutely necessary," the woman said, "is that he should marry me. Otherwise, my dear Edward, your debts will never be paid, and neither will mine!"

"I am well aware of that," said the man who had just spoken. "At the same time, as Roger says, the Chaplain might be difficult, even though we have a Special Licence."

"What are you saying," the woman snapped, "is that Hue might not be able to make the responses. Well, I will make them for him, and once we are married, there will be nothing anyone can do about it, as you very well know!"

Stunned by what she was hearing, Valencia very gently moved the curtain in front of her just a fraction to one side.

She bent forward so that she could see into the Chapel with just one of her eyes.

Standing in the centre of the small aisle of the Chapel itself, which had been built to hold, at the outside, thirty people, she could see a lady.

She thought that she was the most beautiful person imaginable.

Glittering with jewels, she was wearing a red silk gown which accentuated the darkness of her hair.

She seemed to glow like a precious stone against the ancient walls of the Chapel.

The two men standing near her were dressed in the height of fashion.

Because one of them distinctly resembled her in a very masculine manner, Valencia was sure that this was her brother.

He was the "Edward" whose debts had to be paid.

Then, as she looked again, the woman whom she knew must be Lady Hester Stansfield, said:

"It is all planned, and as soon as dinner is over, you carry him in here while the others keep watch so that the servants do not interfere."

She paused, pointing her finger, then went on:

"You, Edward, fetch the Chaplain, or, if you prefer, Roger will go with you. I hear there is an underground passage from here to the Chaplain's House, so no one will see you."

Valencia gave a little gasp.

She was suddenly afraid that they might decide to look for it, in which case they would discover her there listening.

But to her relief, when she was just wondering if she should hurry away, she heard Lady Hester say:

"Well, that being settled, I am going upstairs to rest. Now, listen, Edward, I will go up to my room after dinner, and I will not come down until the Chaplain is here and you have persuaded him that all he has to do is perform the ceremony."

"Would it not be better for you to wait with Dolphinston?" Edward asked.

"No, it would not!" Lady Hester snapped. "You have seen what all the servants are like in this place, nosing about, looking at us as if we were animals from the Zoo. If we are not careful, they will take it upon themselves to interfere."

She paused before she added:

"All you have to do is exactly as I tell you. I have it all planned, and it will take me only a few seconds, once everything is ready, to slip down a secondary staircase which I have found leads almost directly from my bed-room floor to this place."

There was a note of irritation in her voice which made her brother say:

"All right, have it your own way. We will do as you say, but for God's sake, do not make a mess of it! I need the money, and quickly, otherwise I may find myself in prison."

"Leave it to me," Lady Hester replied. "I know exactly what I am doing, and apart from anything else, I shall enjoy being the Countess of Dolphinston. I will certainly make this mouldy old place a damned sight more comfortable than it is at the moment!"

She walked out of the Chapel as she spoke, and Valencia drew in her breath in horror.

For a moment she could hardly believe that she had not only heard a Lady swear, which was shocking enough in itself, but also, incredible though it might be, she had listened to a plot to drug the Earl and then marry him.

Although it was something he himself did not wish for.

He would have no idea that it was happening until it was too late.

'I must save him,' she thought.

She was not certain how she could do so.

She knew only that something, however difficult, had to be done.

chapter two

HUE Dolphin had been completely astonished when he had learned, after his cousins' deaths, that he was heir to the title.

He had been so long in India with his Regiment that he had almost forgotten what things were like in England.

After his father's death he was out of touch with anything that concerned his relations.

Not that he had ever been particularly interested in those who lived at Dolphin Priory.

He had never been in the house, nor had he come in contact with his cousins George and William.

He had heard that one of them had been killed but he had not learned of the death of the other.

So he could hardly believe he was hearing the truth when he was informed by his Commanding Officer that a telegram had been received from the War Office.

It said that his cousin was dead, and informed him of his new position in life.

Hue Dolpin had been brought up very austerely in the extreme North of England, where his father had a small estate.

He spent his days, when he was at home for the holidays, riding over the uncultivated land.

He enjoyed more than anything else the well-bred horses which his father owned.

He had little contact with young people of his own age for the simple reason that there were few neighbours in that particular part of Northumberland.

His father had quarrelled with most of the few there were.

By the time Hue reached the age of sixteen, his father's character had changed considerably.

This was because his wife, of whom he was fond in his own way, had run away with a man fifteen years younger than himself.

She could no longer bear the austerity in which they lived and the authoritarian behaviour of her husband.

When Hue came back from School to find what had happened, his father had begun to indoctrinate him with the idea that all women were treacherous.

They were, he asserted, selfish, concerned only with their own interests, and completely untrustworthy.

At first Hue found it hard to hear his mother being talked of in such a derogatory manner.

Then gradually, as the years passed, he began to

absorb the poisonous attitude of his father into his own thoughts and feelings.

It was only when he went out to India that he had found women attractive.

He soon discovered, however, in the Hill Stations, where the women stayed in the hot weather while their husbands were sweating it out in the plains, that everything his father had said about them was true.

He found that because he was so handsome and attractive, they were promiscuous.

He would not have been human if he had not accepted the favours they offered him.

At the same time, he despised them for being unfaithful to the men they had married.

He had several fiery, passionate affairs with women who professed themselves to be wildly in love with him.

He himself hardly considered it to be a compliment.

As he was continually moving about the country, it was not difficult to terminate these passionate *affaires de coeur*.

They actually made little or no imprint on his character.

He was wholly concerned with his work in the Regiment: the fighting that continually seemed to be taking place in some part of the country, and the part he played in what was known by the Raj as the "Great Game."

The secret information, the manner by which it was obtained, the disguises of which he was a past-master, and, above all, the danger excited him far more than any woman could.

Once he had moved on from the vicinity in which he had made love to a woman, he never thought of her again.

He found himself despising the Subalterns, who, unlike himself, were love-sick.

Sometimes they threatened suicide because they could not marry the woman they loved.

Or else they were forced to leave her because of Regimental orders.

Hue Dolphin thought their feelings were exaggerated, uncontrolled, and certainly undignified.

He found himself thinking of the Indians, who treated their women as playthings of pleasure.

This, he thought, was a much more sensible attitude than that of their conquerors.

"I love you, Hue!" one woman said after another.

The repetition of it began to bore him.

Then, inevitably, they would ask plaintively:

"Why do you not love me? When you leave me I always feel frustrated and afraid I shall never see you again."

When he could not rebut this accusation because it was the truth, they would say:

"What are you looking for? What are you wanting in a woman that I cannot give you?"

There was no answer to this.

Actually, he did not want women in his life at all except when they aroused physically an undeniable fire in him.

Once he was satiated, his mind was immediately on his work again.

Although they did not realise it, to him theirs was a spurious existence.

They did not take second place in his life but actually no place at all.

When it was learnt that Hue Dolphin, for whom every man with whom he served had a real affection, had come into a title and was now an extremely rich man, the congratulations he received from all parts of India were undoubtedly sincere.

"Nobody deserves it more, old man!" his brother officers said to him.

His Colonel, when he said good-bye to him, told him:

"We shall miss you more than I like to say, but I know there are many things you will be asked to do in your new position which will demand your intelligence, your determination, and above all, your courage."

Hue Dolphin had been rather surprised by what he said.

At the same time, as he travelled homewards he thought it unlikely that he would find anything to do that was as intriguing and dangerous as what had monopolised his concentration for the last five years.

As the Suez Canal was open, the voyage from India had taken him only seventeen days.

But that had been long enough for Lady Hester Stansfield.

She had come aboard at Bombay, where she had been staying at Government House.

Her reputation for being one of the most beautiful women in England had preceded her.

There was inevitably a great deal of excitement among those who had boarded the P. and O. Liner at Calcutta.

The Earl had heard them talking about Lady Hester, but had not taken any particular interest.

He was, in fact, studying the history of the Dolphin family in a book which had been sent to him somewhat belatedly by one of his relatives.

He had found it waiting for him at the Viceroy's house.

The letter which accompanied it said:

I thought you would like to read this, if you have not already done so, and it comes to you with affectionate greetings from your cousin

Amy

He had not the slightest idea who his cousin Amy might be.

He supposed it was kind of her to have sent him a history of the family.

Then he thought somewhat sarcastically that none of his Dolphin relatives had taken any interest in him until now.

He had known they were a large family and that the Fifth Earl was the head of it.

His father, however, had always despised his cousin, saying he had no use for anyone who was so stuck-up and thought too much of his own consequence.

It was only when Hue started to read their history that he realised how much the Dolphins had contributed to England.

They had served their Sovereign brilliantly, whether as Statesmen or as soldiers.

In fact, by the time he had finished the book, of which he had read every word, he wished that he had made it his business when he was in England to visit Dolphin Priory.

It had been made over to the family on the Dissolution of the Monasteries in the time of Henry VIII.

If he had gone there, he would have made the acquaintance of the late Earl.

He had, however, no time for retrospection after Lady Hester swept into his life like a whirlwind.

She had already decided before she boarded the Liner at Bombay that the most important man on the passenger list was the new Earl of Dolphinston.

She told him that she knew his family and was ready to help him in any way possible.

She then proceeded to make it very obvious that, title or no title, she found him attractive as a man.

She would, he was well aware, be disappointed if he did not reciprocate her advances.

The Earl would have been completely inhuman if he had not been flattered by her attention, and also indeed captivated by her charms.

She was very beautiful and different in every way from any of the women he had met and made love to in India.

To begin with, Lady Hester was extremely sophisticated.

She moved in the Society in London which defied the pomposity and parochialism of the Queen. It concentrated on enjoying itself to the exclusion of everything else.

Her attractiveness was not only confined to the beauty of her face.

Being determined that every man should fall at her feet, Lady Hester had learnt the sciences of love, in the same way that the Courtesans of Paris had learnt to use them to their advantage.

She aroused the Earl in a manner that he would not have believed possible.

Although he thought cynically that she behaved more like a scarlet woman than a Lady, he found himself unable to ignore the fires she ignited in him.

In fact, she had a sensuous, seductive, exotic fascination about her.

It led to the Earl's spending most of his days and nights on the voyage in Lady Hester's cabin.

He knew as she wound herself round him physically and mentally that he had for the moment no wish to be free of her.

When they arrived in London, Lady Hester took over.

The moment she saw Dolphin House in Park Lane she made compelling excuses for having nowhere to lay her head, and became the Earl's guest.

She arranged to be chaperoned by her younger brother, the Honorable Edward Ward.

He moved in with an eagerness which would have made the Earl suspicious if he had been aware of it.

Lady Hester convinced him that they were doing him a kindness in introducing him to the best of Society.

Besides helping in running his house, she entertained when he was so much in demand not only with the Secretary of State for India, but also with the Prince of Wales.

It was natural that the Earl found it a compliment

that the heir to the throne should wish to talk to him about India and appeared to have a liking for his company.

He was also sent for by the Queen, who professed a great love of the latest addition to her Empire.

She encouraged him to talk about what was happening in the country to which he had devoted the last five years of his life.

He found Her Majesty well-informed, especially as to the menace of the Russians on the North-West Frontier.

She was aware of the difficulties raised by Indian customs such as *suttee* and other unpleasant practices, which the British were trying to stamp out.

"You are such a success, dearest!" Lady Hester cooed at him when he returned from Windsor, "and I have arranged for you to meet several important Statesmen at a dinner-party you are giving tomorrow evening."

The party also included a number of Lady Hester's special friends who were as alluring and seductive as she was herself.

They made the Earl feel as if he had stepped into a strange world of which he knew nothing.

At the same time, at the back of his mind, he was well aware that the Prince of Wales was indulging in illicit love-affairs.

This was, to his surprise, known to the whole nation.

Lady Hester's friends were all married to complacent husbands either with interests in other parts of the country, or deeply involved with some other lovely lady.

When he thought about it, he knew that his father had been right.

Women were not only promiscuous and untrustworthy, but in many ways despicable.

It made him even more determined than he had been before that he would never marry.

It was something he had decided a long time ago.

His first love-affair was in Simla with a very attractive woman whose husband was with his Regiment in the South of India.

She had fallen very much in love with him.

As they lay side by side in one of the small bungalows built round the Viceroy's House, which was extremely convenient for lovers, she had said:

"I cannot lose you! How can I go back to Robert, feeling as I do about you?"

She had moved a little closer to him and said in a whisper:

"Let us run away together. I know it would mean your leaving the Regiment, but you would never regret it, for I would make you very, very happy."

For a moment Hue Dolphin could hardly believe what he was hearing.

It had never struck him for one moment that any woman would want to endure the social ostracism and the vulgarity of the Divorce Court for him.

Then he was aware that the last thing he wanted was to retire and spend the rest of his life with this clinging creature to whom he had just made love.

He had found her attractive.

For a few minutes the sensations she had aroused in him had been very gratifying.

But now he had no particular feelings about her

except that of physical satisfaction and a desire to go to sleep.

It had, however, required all his tact and a great many insincere compliments to make her realise how cruel it would be to leave her husband.

When he got back to his own bed-room he told himself that in the future he would be much more careful.

He must certainly avoid women whose temperaments made them mentally unstable.

He, therefore, made sure that those with whom he was subsequently involved were what his fellow-officers called "up to scratch."

They had no ideas beyond the passing pleasure of the moment.

Once or twice there were tearful scenes when he parted from some lovely woman whom he had made very happy and whom he had enjoyed physically.

They had, however, never touched his heart, supposing that he had one!

On his return to England he found Lady Hester genuinely useful.

It had certainly simplified matters when she had not only introduced him to what she called the "right people," but warned him against those who were wrong.

They were, as she put it, only out to make use of him because he was a new "Social Lion" whom every hostess wanted to capture.

"You must learn to be discriminating, darling," Lady Hester had said when they were alone. "The Social World is full of snares for those who do not know it well."

"I am fortunate to have you to guide me," the Earl said.

"I want you to think that, and you know all I want is to make you happy and the success you undoubtedly are."

The Earl found it very enjoyable.

But he was also uncomfortably aware that while he was giving a considerable amount of his time to the needs of the Empire, he had not yet considered the people he employed, nor visited Dolphin Priory, the house which had featured very prominently in the history of the family.

Several of his relatives had approached him while he was in London.

While they insisted on entertaining him, he had to admit that they did not fit in with Lady Hester's friends.

Because he was very perceptive, he was also aware, and it amused him, that they seemed to be shocked by Lady Hester.

His women relatives considered her "fast," but he put it down to jealousy.

Lady Hester herself said that a number of the more stuffy, traditional hostesses resented her position in the Prince of Wales's circle of close friends.

"They are known," she told him, "as 'The Marlborough House Set.'"

The Earl was quite prepared to agree that they were more amusing, and certainly more decorative, than the people he had met at parties to which he had been invited by his relations.

In fact, he found that the majority of his women cousins were plain and rather dowdy.

The men, in most cases, were very much older than himself.

They seemed determined to "lay down the law" about everything and everybody without listening to his opinion in the matter.

It was, therefore, a relief after a long day at the Foreign Office to find himself laughing. The witty innuendoes made the conversation of Lady Hester and her friends sparkle like jewels.

As party succeeded party in the big Dining-Room in Park Lane, he found it was impossible to leave London.

There were so many engagements already filling his diary.

When at last, almost too late, he realised the danger he was in, it came like a bomb-shell.

Lady Hester, lying naked in his arms, her dark hair falling against his chest, had said:

"You know, my dearest, that people are talking about us, and I think we ought to do something about it."

The Earl was feeling sleepy and he asked without thinking:

"What do you expect me to do?"

"I should have thought that was obvious," Lady Hester said softly, "and, darling, we will be very, very happy together."

For a moment he did not take it in.

Then just as when he was in India, some perceptive part of his brain warned him of danger.

Instantly he was alert and wide-awake.

It was as if his eyes had been blinded but were now suddenly clear.

He was aware that while Lady Hester amused him and he had found her, as he thought, very useful, he had no wish whatsoever to marry her.

Nor, for that matter, had he any wish to marry anybody else.

His father's condemnation of women had been ingrained in him ever since he was a boy.

Now it all came flooding back into his consciousness.

He realised all too clearly that women were contemptible.

The idea of being married to Lady Hester was completely horrifying.

They had been together long enough now for him to have no illusions about the way in which she deliberately excited him.

Also the way she contrived to make him pay a great number of her bills.

She would show him accounts for things she had bought on his behalf.

He was shrewd enough to suspect that these had been falsified so as to add up to an inflated sum, part of which would go into her own pocket.

He paid because he could afford it; to do so was easier than having a scene.

But now he knew that while at the moment he had no wish to be rid of Lady Hester, he had no intention of having her permanently in his life.

In fact, he could not imagine a worse fate than being married to her.

What was more, although he had not wished to admit it to himself until now, his desire for her as a woman was not as intense as it had been when they first met on the voyage back from India.

"I have been a fool!" he told himself.

Then all his experience and training in how to evade danger came to his rescue.

He kissed Lady Hester before he said:

"I must go to my own bed, my dear. I am so tired that I can hardly think straight, and the only person I can blame for that is you!"

"I have made you happy?" Lady Hester asked in a soft voice.

"I will talk about that tomorrow," he replied, yawning as he spoke.

Setting her on one side, he got out of bed.

She gave a little cry of protest and put out her arms to try to hold him to her, saying:

"You have not answered my suggestion!"

The Earl yawned again.

"What suggestion?" he asked.

Then, as he put on a long velvet robe which was very much more expensive than anything he had ever owned before, he said:

"God, I am tired! I find it difficult to remember anything except that you are a very beautiful woman!"

"That is what I want you to think," Lady Hester said, "and that is why—"

He interrupted her by yawning once again.

Then, before she could hold his attention, he had opened the door.

"Good-night, Hester," he said, "if you do not sleep well, I shall take it as an insult."

He heard her give a soft laugh.

Then he closed the door and walked quickly down the dimly-lit passage to his own bedroom.

Only when he reached it did he ask himself how he could have been so obtuse as not to have suspected that Hester might wish to marry him.

It had never occurred to him that as she was a widow and she and her brother were both, as he now knew, extremely hard-up, the prospect of becoming the Countess of Dolphinston would be irresistible.

Now he could see only too clearly where she had been leading him.

Like a stupid greenhorn he had followed her into what he was aware was an appalling threat to his freedom.

She had established herself very comfortably in Park Lane.

She was astute enough not to have only her brother as a chaperon. Under one pretext or another she filled the house continually with her own friends.

They were delighted to stay in a house where they could welcome their current paramour as a guest not only at meals but in their bed-rooms.

Some were impoverished but titled relatives of Lady Hester's. They wanted a comfortable place to stay when they came to London from the country for their shopping.

It had all seemed quite natural and above-board to the Earl.

Now he realised that Lady Hester had made it quite clear that she was his hostess.

Most people would naturally assume in the circumstances that sooner or later their engagement would be announced.

When he had first met Lady Hester aboard the ship, she still had three months of conventional mourning to do for her late husband.

The Earl learned later, she had been separated from him for a year before his death.

There was nothing legal about it, they had just gone their own ways.

"Because," Lady Hester had said, "we were completely incompatible!"

But she was free to marry again and who could be more suitable than himself?

"Why could I not have realised it sooner?" the Earl asked himself now.

He walked about his room for a short while before finally he got into bed.

He did not sleep, but lay in the darkness thinking of what he could do, and finding the question difficult to answer.

It was finally seven o'clock in the morning when he rang for his valet.

He told him he wanted to see Mr. Stevenson, the secretary, who had been with the late Earl.

He had already found him very useful and very knowledgeable about the various estates.

It was with Mr. Stevenson that he now arranged to go to the country.

He then empowered him to inform Lady Hester when she woke that he was leaving London.

He had hoped she would not want to go with him.

He had, however, not been particularly surprised, when the carriage came to the door to take him to the station, to find that she was there, too, and ready to travel with him.

She was, however, too clever to reproach him.

Also, she was far too astute even to seem surprised at his sudden departure.

"How can you have such a wonderful idea that we should go to the country?" She smiled up at him. "And just when there was really nothing exciting to do this week-end!"

"As I shall be very busy exploring Dolphin Priory and inspecting the estate," the Earl replied, "I think you would be happier staying in London."

"I am never happy unless I am with you," Lady Hester said pointedly, "and as I am determined that neither of us shall be bored, I have invited a small party to join us at the Priory."

The Earl drew in his breath.

He said nothing as Lady Hester reeled off the names of several of her particular friends.

He noted that her brother, Edward, and Sir Roger Crawford, a somewhat dissolute man who always wanted to gamble for high stakes, were included.

"I wish you had asked me before inviting all these people," he said with a touch of irritation in his voice. "I have so much to do at the Priory that I really shall have no time to entertain anybody."

Lady Hester had clasped her hands together in contrition.

"Oh, dearest, how terrible of me! But I was only thinking of you, and had no idea that you wanted to be on your own. What shall I do? I cannot put them off now when they have already left for the station!"

The Earl realised there was nothing he could do without being extremely rude.

He had every wish to avoid precipitating a scene.

He then told himself that the best thing he could do was to make sure on their return to London that Lady Hester did not stay, as she would expect to, with him any longer.

It was too soon to tell her so yet.

He could only hope the week-end would not be too difficult.

He had every intention of spending his time not only exploring the Priory which he had never seen, but also inspecting the farms.

He would make himself acquainted with all the other activities on the estate.

He had learned about it all from the excellent reports sent him regularly by his Manager, a man called Rawlins, ever since he inherited.

He had the idea that the Priory was going to be a place he would not only be proud of, but which, in the future, would be his home.

He chided himself for having spent so long in London.

It was not only because of Lady Hester and her entertainments.

There was so much the Foreign Office had wanted to learn from him and then discuss fully.

There had also been so many people the Foreign Secretary had wished him to meet that he had, in fact, been kept genuinely busy.

So much so that Lady Hester had protested about it.

They drove in his comfortable carriage to the station.

At short notice Mr. Stevenson had managed to have his private coach attached to the train.

The Earl was thinking he had to be on his guard.

It was not difficult to imagine Lady Hester behaving like a wild animal who might maim him at any moment.

He was aware, with his perception that was more acute than most people's, that she was, in fact, considerably perturbed by his sudden decision to leave London and herself.

She was calculating how she could enslave him.

She was determined to make certain that he would offer her what she wanted more than anything else— a simple wedding-ring.

Almost as if she read his thoughts, Lady Hester slipped her arm through his and said in her soft, beguiling voice:

"It is exciting, is it not, Hue dearest, for you to be going home? For that is what the Priory means to every Dolphin, wherever he may be."

She paused for a moment.

"For you especially it will mean the home you have not had since your father died, but which I have longed to make for you."

The Earl was fortunately saved from having to reply to this transparent innuendo.

At that moment Edward Ward and Sir Roger Crawford appeared on the platform and entered the private coach.

"This is a surprise, Dolphin!" Edward Ward said in a hearty voice. "I had no idea you were thinking of going to the country until I received Hester's note. Of course I understand. You want to see your future home, and show it to Hester."

The way he spoke, with a menacing look in his

dark eyes, made the Earl feel as if the prison-bars were already encircling him.

The door was being closed and locked so that there could be no escape.

With a tremendous effort he managed to laugh, as if Edward had said something funny.

But he told himself grimly that however uncomfortable the show-down might be, whatever the accusations made against him, he would not in any circumstances and whatever the pressure marry Lady Hester!

chapter three

LADY Hester left the Chapel, the two men following her.

Valencia hurried back down the secret passage to the house.

She was thinking wildly about what she could do to save the Earl.

Also, she had to prevent her father from being threatened, as Lady Hester had suggested.

It seemed incredible that a Lady should think of anything so horrifying.

She had, however, understood from the hard determination in Lady Hester's voice that she would let nothing prevent her from marrying the Earl.

As Valencia reached the door that led into her own house, she decided that it would be a great mistake to tell her father what was happening.

He would inevitably be extremely upset.

He would undoubtedly protest very strenuously against marrying a man who was incapable of making his responses.

In which case, they would try to intimidate him, and even man-handle him.

"Who else can I turn to?" Valencia asked.

There were only two servants in the house, one being her old Nanny, who was getting on for seventy.

She was still a tower of strength in any emergency when it concerned children or those she loved.

Yet she was obviously not capable of standing up to Lady Hester and her brother.

The other was a general servant in the shape of Emily, who could not be relied upon.

Being a girl from the village, if anything untoward happened, she would immediately tell her family, who would relate it to everybody else.

"What can I do? What can I do?" Valencia murmured, and it was in reality a prayer.

Then she remembered Ben.

Ben was the man who looked after their horses.

Although he was not as young as he had been when he first came to the Chaplain's House, he was extremely strong and very trustworthy.

Also, he had known Valencia since she was very young.

He was, she knew, extremely fond of her, and would do anything she asked of him.

What was more, he was a man of few words and he would certainly not gossip to anyone if she asked him to keep silent.

She hurried across the hall, out through the front-door, then down to the stables.

There were only three horses there to be looked after by Ben.

He spent the rest of his day working in the garden, where Valencia helped him when she had the time.

Now he was putting fresh straw down in the stall which housed her beloved "Swallow."

He was a horse she had owned since he was a foal and had been given to her by the late Earl.

A beautiful animal, well-bred, and because she had taught him with love, he responded to her every wish.

At the sight of her, he whinnied and moved forward away from Ben so that he was waiting as she opened the door.

She stroked his nose and patted his neck before she said:

"I want to talk to you, Ben, and it is very important!"

He did not seem surprised, he merely ran his hand over Swallow's silky coat.

Then he followed Valencia from the stall out into the passage.

Quickly, in as few words as possible, she told him what she had overheard.

Ben listened without interruption, then said in his slow voice:

"If ye asks me, Miss Valencia, that be real wicked!"

"That is what I thought you would think, Ben," Valencia said. "What we have to do is to take the Earl away from the Chapel before the ceremony can take place and hide him until he is well enough to stand up for himself."

"Now, 'ow can we do that, Miss Valencia?" Ben asked.

"This is where we use the Priests' Hole," Valencia replied. "You may not be aware of it, but there are secret passages in the house which were built in order to hide the Royalists from Oliver Cromwell's Roundheads."

She paused before continuing:

"And before that there were Priests' Holes where the Roman Catholic priests could hide when they were being persecuted by Queen Elizabeth."

Valencia was not quite certain how much of this Ben absorbed, but he was listening intently as she went on:

"These secret places are supposed to be known only to the Master of the house, but years ago, when I was a child, I was shown the Priests' Hole in the Chapel by my cousin George."

"So—it's in t'Chapel," Ben said slowly.

"Yes, behind the altar," Valencia answered, "and this is what I suggest we do. . . ."

She talked to Ben for another ten minutes, making him repeat her instructions so that there could be no mistake.

Then she went back to the house.

She felt as if the quiet, peaceful world she had known all her life had suddenly become strange, menacing, and very frightening.

How was it possible that there could be beautiful women like Lady Hester who would marry a man by a trick, simply because she wanted his money?

And how could the Earl, who had inherited anything so magnificent as the Priory and also had won medals for gallantry, be involved with people who were prepared to do anything, however wrong, at her request?

It seemed to Valencia as if all that had been familiar was in confusion.

She was suddenly confronted with the evil against which her father preached.

It had never seemed real until now.

It was like the fairy-stories she had read as a child, where to save a helpless damsel the wicked Ogre or a fire-breathing dragon had to be disposed of. Usually by a Knight in Shining Armour, or else by Prince Charming.

But now the roles were reversed.

'I am the only person, beside those three people from London, who knows what is about to happen,' she thought.

It suddenly struck her that she might, if she were brave enough, ask to see the Earl and tell him what was going to occur.

Then she was quite certain that in the first place he would not believe her.

If it were announced by the servants that his Chaplain's daughter wished to speak to him, Lady Hester would either prevent it or make quite certain her story was laughed to scorn.

Either way, Lady Hester, her brother, and their friend would doubtless try to enslave the Earl on some other occasion.

If it happened in London, she would not be there to save him.

"The only thing I can do," Valencia told herself, "is to hide him in the Priests' Hole."

She paused before continuing:

"Then when he is well enough to confront Lady Hester with her plot, he will surely be able to fight his own battles."

She would then at least have the collaboration of her father.

He would be able to swear that he had been fetched to the chapel.

Only to find when he arrived that there was no bridegroom waiting as Lady Hester had intended there should be.

At the same time, the whole thing was very frightening.

It would be hard to behave normally and not make her father suspicious there was anything wrong.

Then she changed into the simple muslin gown she usually wore when they were alone together.

Her fingers were trembling so much that she found it difficult to do up the buttons which had never caused her any trouble in the past.

They ate a small meal, cooked by Nanny, and brought into the Dining-Room by Emily, who waited on them rather inadequately.

The food was plain but good.

Yet Valencia found it hard to swallow anything that was on her plate.

Although her father did not notice, she also found it difficult to concentrate on what he was saying.

They always had the most interesting conversations at meal-times.

Not only was the Reverend Matthew Hadley an extremely erudite man, but he was clever enough to translate books.

These were the delight of scholars, derived from ancient Greek manuscripts and from papyrus found in tombs in Egypt.

This meant he was continually in touch with other scholars who were concerned with the same work as he was.

Valencia found his translations fascinating.

He was telling her that he was now translating a description of the services which took place in the Temples in Athens, another on the predictions of the Oracle at Delphi.

"How exciting, Papa!" she managed to gasp.

"I have not got very far as yet with the latter," her father explained, and paused before he continued:

"But I know you will be delighted with what has been divulged so far, which is very much more explicit than anything that has been uncovered before."

"You know how thrilling it will be for me to read it," Valencia said.

She feared her father was gong to suggest that she go with him to his Study after dinner, and added quickly:

"Perhaps tomorrow we might have dinner a little earlier, then you can read me everything you have done so far."

"I would enjoy that," her father said with a smile. "I am very lucky to have such a clever daughter who understands how important this work is."

"I am sure, Papa, that after this they will offer you a position as Professor at one of the Universities."

The Vicar looked surprised, as if that had never occurred to him. Then he said:

"Would that please you, Valencia? I often think it

is very dull for you living here so quietly, now that since your mother's death we see so few people, and you are never invited to parties or Balls."

"I am very happy with you, Papa. In fact, I am not certain I would want to leave the Priory. Yet it would be a great honour for you to be given a chair at Oxford."

For a moment her father looked pleased, then he said:

"Let us not be over-optimistic in case we are disappointed."

Valencia gave a little laugh as she rose from the table, saying:

"I am sure that is very wise, Papa, but being hopeful costs nothing, and I shall certainly pray that you will be rewarded, as you should be."

Her father placed his hand affectionately on her shoulder as they walked together from the Dining-Room.

Then as he went to his Study, Valencia knew that in a few minutes he would be immersed in his work.

He would be quite unaware of time and not in the least curious as to what she was doing.

She knew she had to join Ben, who would be waiting for her near the door which led into the underground passage.

She put a shawl round her shoulders in case, as she suspected, the Priests' Hole, which was deep down under the ground, was cold.

Then, avoiding the kitchen, where Nanny and Emily would be washing up, she slipped from the house.

As she expected, Ben was waiting for her.

Without saying anything to each other, they hurried down the underground passage, stopping only to go more slowly before they entered the Chapel.

Valencia was half-afraid that something might have gone wrong.

Either the Earl was already there, or Lady Hester had changed her plans.

As she entered the Vestry she was aware that somebody had lit the candles on the altar.

Also the larger ones which stood on either side of it on magnificent ornate silver stands which had been presented to a former Earl by the City of London had been lit.

Moving cautiously, she crossed the Vestry.

She peered through the curtain, as she had done earlier in the day, and saw that there was nobody in the Chapel.

She beckoned to Ben, who was following her, and they moved behind the altar.

The altar was a large slab of pink marble which stood on supports that had been carved by a master craftsman.

Valencia, however, could not see them because the altar was covered with a cloth.

It had been embroidered by a previous Countess of Dolphin a century ago.

There was plenty of room for Valencia and Ben to sit below and behind the altar.

They could be seen only if somebody crept around the back, which was not really likely.

Immediately behind the altar, set cleverly into the stone-flagged floor so that it was completely unnoticeable unless one knew of its existence, was the entrance to the Priests' Hole.

As Valencia knew, it was easy for a man to raise one flagstone.

It would reveal an opening leading straight down underground by way of a ladder attached to the wall.

She knew this would be impossible for the Earl to negotiate if he was unconscious.

She, therefore, signalled to Ben to open it up so that he could see what was expected of him.

She showed him the place where he could release the catch and pull back the heavy stone.

Then, after he had looked down into the darkness, she handed him the lantern.

She had carried it in her hand as they had walked down the underground passage.

Ben understood without words what was required.

Swiftly he descended into the Priests' Hole down the vertical ladder.

When he reached the bottom he set down the lantern.

It revealed to him the small room where many priests must have hidden and saved their lives in the past.

There was an austere wooden bedstead against one wall, a small altar against another with a silver crucifix standing on it, and two unlit candles.

In the past there must have been more candles, Valencia had always thought.

Perhaps also as fine an altar-cloth as the one in the Chapel upstairs.

These had obviously been removed for one reason or another over the centuries.

Yet the Priests' Hole itself had survived to be once again a useful hiding place.

Ben took only a quick glance around, then, leaving the lantern, climbed back up the ladder.

He put the flagstone back into place and joined Valencia.

She was sitting under the altar with her knees doubled up under her and her back against the marble support.

There was no sound.

Yet to Valencia there was the atmosphere she had always found in the Chapel.

It was as if the many generations of Dolphins who had worshipped there had left their faith to vibrate for those who still came to pray.

Valencia went to the Chapel whenever she felt upset or depressed.

She had also gone there with her joys and happiness.

She felt nearer to God in the Chapel than in the Village Church.

Sometimes after her mother's death she had been sure, as she knelt to pray in one of the ancient carved pews, that her mother was there beside her.

She found herself praying now, as her mother had taught her, for help in rescuing the Earl.

"After all, Mama," she said, "you are a Dolphin and we cannot allow one of your family to be treated in such a despicable and horrible way."

She had often thought that when she knew the Earl, as she hoped she would, she would tell him that her mother had been a second cousin of the late Earl.

Also, that her father had been a first cousin of the Earl before him.

It was shown, if one looked for it, in the family tree, and she wondered if the new Earl would be interested.

Perhaps he would be content just to be in such an important position himself and have no interest in the other members of his family.

It had certainly seemed that way, considering he had not come down to the Priory since his return to England.

Not even to inspect his property and call on the farmers.

Or, as everybody had hoped he would, to meet those who worked for him.

Instead, he had been busy entertaining his personal guests. If they were all like Lady Hester, they were totally incompatible with his neighbours in the country.

And certainly incompatible with the families who had served his forebears dutifully for many generations.

"I must not be critical," Valencia told herself.

She knew it was what her father would say to her if she revealed to him what was in her thoughts.

Even so, she could not help feeling angry that the Earl should have chosen as friends people who behaved like Lady Hester, her brother, and the other man in the party called Roger.

"I hate them!" Valencia said beneath her breath.

But she was ashamed at having such un-Christian thoughts when she was in a House of God.

It was then she heard footsteps in the distance.

A moment later she was aware that two men had entered the chapel by the door from the house.

She was certain from the heavy way in which they were walking that they were carrying the Earl with them.

She heard them tramping slowly up the short aisle.

Then they were setting down their burden in a chair.

She had noticed as she entered the Chapel that it had been moved from the Chancel, where it normally stood beside the altar.

It was a chair intended for use by the Archbishop or any other ecclesiastic of great importance.

When she had seen it set in front of the pews directly by the altar-steps she had guessed for whom it was intended.

Then she heard Edward Ward say in a low voice:

"He will be all right there. You go and fetch Hester, and I will collect the Chaplain. I only hope he has not gone to bed!"

"At this hour?" Roger questioned.

"My dear boy, you are in the country now and the inhabitants go to roost with the birds!"

He spoke in a derisive tone.

Valencia heard the other man laugh before he walked back the way they had come.

Edward Ward, on the other hand, hurried to the Vestry.

She heard him opening the door that led into the underground passage.

He paused and she thought perhaps he was surprised to find it so dark.

There were, however, small windows like arrow-slits which let in a certain amount of light.

Now the moon was rising up the sky and even without a lantern he should be able to find his way, she thought.

Valencia held her breath.

If he waited too long, Lady Hester might come into the Chapel before she and Ben had time to remove the Earl.

Then, as his footsteps died away, they moved from their hiding-place.

The Earl was sitting, as Valencia expected, in the Archbishop's chair, his arms hanging limply on either side of it.

She glanced at him, and realised that he was just as handsome as she had expected him to be.

But his eyes were closed, his legs were stuck out in front of him, and he was obviously completely unconscious.

Ben put his hands under his shoulders and Valencia picked up his legs.

It took them only a minute to carry the Earl round to the back of the altar.

Valencia hurried down the ladder into the Priests' Hole below.

As she had already arranged with Ben, he lowered the Earl slowly down to her.

First she could hold his ankles, then his knees.

When Ben lay flat on the ground, he managed to lower the Earl still farther until Valencia held him in her arms.

He was very heavy, so she made no attempt to move.

She waited until Ben had replaced the stone flag and hurried down the ladder to take the Earl from her.

Between them they got him onto the bed.

Because she could not help being curious as to what would happen when the others came back, Valencia climbed up the ladder.

Her head just touched the stone which covered the entrance to the Priests' Hole, and she listened.

First there was just silence, until she heard footsteps at the back of the Chapel.

In a voice that sounded hard and astonished she heard Lady Hester exclaim:

"Where is Hue? You said you had left him here."

"He was in that chair," Sir Roger said, "and quite unconscious."

"He could not have been!" Lady Hester retorted. "How could you and Edward have been such fools as not to make the drug strong enough?"

"All I can say is that it was double what you told us to use. In fact, I thought Edward was overdoing it!"

"If that was so, it would be impossible for him to move far!" Lady Hester snapped.

At that moment Valencia heard her father's voice, and a second later Edward Ward said:

"Now, here is Lady Hester, Vicar, waiting for us, and my friend, Sir Roger Crawford."

Then before either of the two people he had introduced could respond, he exclaimed:

"Where is the Earl?"

"That is just what I was asking!" Lady Hester answered.

"He was here when we left, you know he was, Edward!" Sir Roger asserted.

"Of course he was!" Edward Ward replied. "I put him into this chair myself!"

"How could anyone make such a muddle of anything so simple except an abject fool?" Lady Hester asked angrily.

Listening, Valencia could visualise her father looking with surprise and consternation at the three people bickering with each other.

"Well, anyway," Edward Ward said, "he cannot have gone far. If he got out of the chair, he has very likely collapsed in the passage. We had better go to look for him."

He must have turned towards the door, because Valencia heard her father say in his quiet, well-modulated voice:

"Are you saying, Mr. Ward, that His Lordship is unwell? I had no idea he was indisposed in any way."

"He is not as healthy as one might wish," Edward Ward said quickly, "but he was very eager to be married, there is no doubt about that!"

"Yes, of course he is!" Lady Hester said, as if she realised she must reassure the Vicar.

She paused, looking concerned before continuing:

"It was the Earl himself who planned that we should be married tonight, and naturally, he wanted you, his own Chaplain, to officiate."

Her father did not reply.

Valencia knew he must be baffled and somewhat concerned by this extraordinary scene.

As if he felt he was expected to take charge, Edward Ward said:

"We had better look for His Lordship. Come on, Roger, nobody could hide here unless he is behind the altar!"

He must have walked past her father and moved behind the altar as he spoke.

Valencia could hear his footsteps, loud and heavy on the flagstones.

The rest of the Chapel was carpeted, and as he moved away, his feet sounded softer and not, she thought, so aggressive.

"Well, I suppose the only thing I can do," Lady Hester said petulantly, "is to wait, but I consider it extremely inconvenient that the Earl should disappear in this extraordinary manner!"

"Perhaps, Your Ladyship, it would be wiser to wait until the morning," the Vicar said quietly.

He looked at her before he continued:

"I always think that marriage is a Sacrament that should not be treated lightly, nor should it, unless it is absolutely necessary, take place late in the evening."

"That is when the Earl wanted it to be, and I intend to become his wife tonight!" Lady Hester said sharply.

"Then, of course, the only thing we can do is to wait," the Vicar said gently. "Perhaps you will excuse me if, while we are doing so, I say my prayers."

He must have moved away from Lady Hester, Valencia thought, and was now kneeling in front of the altar.

She knew by the intonation in her father's voice that by now his surprise had changed to apprehension.

He was aware that something untoward was happening and required Divine guidance.

Because she loved him, Valencia longed for him to know that everything was all right.

She had, in fact, saved the Earl.

But she prayed, as she knew he was praying, that God would prevent the new owner of Dolphin Priory from coming to any physical or spiritual harm.

It was about five minutes before she heard Edward Ward and Sir Roger come back into the Chapel.

They were moving quickly and did not speak until they were beside Lady Hester, who was now sitting in the Archbishop's chair.

"There is no sign of him anywhere!" they reported.

"I do not believe it!" Lady Hester said angrily. "Where have you looked?"

"In practically every room on the Ground Floor," her brother answered.

"I assure you, Hester," Sir Roger joined in, "it would be quite impossible for Hue to have left this Chapel on his own and to have walked up the stairs."

"It is all very well to say that," Lady Hester objected angrily, "but if he is not here, then where is he?"

She glared at them before she went on:

"Who could possibly have spirited him away? Anyway, who knew of our plan except ourselves? Have you been talking, Roger?"

"No, of course not!" he replied. "Why should I, and to whom?"

"Then all I can say is that you two are the biggest

bunglers I have ever met in my whole life!" Lady Hester declared.

She paused before she continued sharply:

"You could not have given him a large enough dose, or it would have been impossible for him to move on his own!"

"I agree with you," Edward Ward said, "and that is why I am quite certain that somebody has taken him out of the Chapel, perhaps as a joke, or perhaps just to spite you."

"If that is true, then find him!" Lady Hester screamed. "And if it is somebody staying here with us, I will kill them!"

Her voice rang out round the Chapel.

Valencia was not surprised when she heard her father's voice:

"I must ask you, My Lady, and you, gentlemen, to remember that you are in a House of God, and not to desecrate it, as you are doing at the moment!"

He stopped for a moment to look at them.

"I am now returning to my own house. If His Lordship requires my services within the next hour before I retire to bed, I suggest you ask him to come himself and tell me of his wishes."

He paused, shaking his head before continuing:

"I find it hard to believe in view of what has happened that he really desires to be married."

The Vicar spoke with dignity and with an authority which left the three people listening to him silent.

Then Valencia heard him walk into the Vestry and knew he was on his way home.

Lady Hester must have waited for the sound of the door closing behind him before she said:

"Now he is suspicious that something is wrong! How could you have been such utter and complete idiots as to let this happen?"

"We only followed your instructions," Edward Ward said sulkily, "and if Hue is on his guard, there may not now be another opportunity."

"There has to be!" Lady Hester said. "Do you hear me—there has to be! I do not believe that you have searched for him properly."

She paused, and then went on:

"In my opinion, he had struggled out of here and collapsed somewhere in a corner, or perhaps he felt the need of air and went out into the garden."

"The garden!" Sir Roger repeated. "I had not thought of that! That is where he will be!"

He was eager as he continued:

"He was bemused by what we had given him and he must have wandered into the Chaplain's garden, or even into his house."

"It is certainly an idea," Edward Ward agreed.

"I tell you what we will do," Sir Roger said. "You, Hester, go and look in the house to see if you can find him there. Edward and I will search the garden, then we will search the Chaplain's house, just to see if he wandered in there."

"Very well," Lady Hester agreed, "but you had better find him one way or another, or I swear I will murder you both, you incompetent fools!"

There was the tap-tap of her high-heeled shoes as she walked down the aisle towards the door which led into the house.

The two men must have watched her go before Edward Ward said:

"Come on, then. I know the way into the garden, and you are probably right, Roger. After what we made him drink, he was very likely longing for fresh air."

They moved away, and Valencia knew what she must do.

She descended the ladder to where Ben was sitting beside the Earl as he lay still and almost lifeless on the priest's bed.

"Stay here, Ben," she said in a whisper. "I must go back to the house, as they are going to search it, but as soon as they have gone, I will return."

He nodded to show he understood.

Valencia climbed up again, and with a tremendous effort managed to push open the flagstone.

She crept out of the Priests' Hole, closed it, and, moving across the Vestry to the underground passage, ran home.

She thought that by now Nanny would have retired to bed, leaving Emily alone in the kitchen.

She slipped up the stairs to her own room.

Pulling off her gown, she put on a pretty muslin negligee that her mother had given her.

She then unpinned her hair.

She went to the door and opened it just a fraction so that she could hear if anything happened downstairs.

Five minutes later there was a sharp knock on the front-door.

Emily could not have heard it, for there was no movement from the kitchen.

Valencia was certain that her father, lost in his

translation of the Greek, was quite oblivious to anything that happened around him.

The knock came again, and now, slowly, Emily came from the kitchen and crossed the hall.

She opened the door and Valencia heard Edward Ward say:

"Has the Vicar retired to bed?"

"No, Sir, he be in t'Study."

"Then we will not disturb him," Edward Ward replied. "But I have his permission to look round the house for somebody who is lost."

"Lost, Sir?"

"You heard what I said. Now, you be a good girl and go back to where you have come from, and do not worry your head over us."

Valencia knew that Emily was too frightened to argue with anyone who spoke in such a commanding manner.

Quickly she shut the door and went to her dressing-table. Sitting down on the stool in front of the mirror, Valencia began to brush her hair.

It was only a few minutes later that there was a knock on her door and at the same time it was opened.

She turned round in astonishment.

Then, seeing two men in the doorway, she rose to her feet, holding the hair-brush in one hand.

"Who . . . are you? What do you . . . want?" she enquired, and hoped her voice sounded frightened.

"It is all right," Edward Ward said soothingly. "I imagine you are the Chaplain's daughter."

"Yes . . . I am," Valencia said, "but you will find . . . my father . . . in his study."

"We know that. We have his permission to look through the house for someone who has got lost."

"Lost?"

"From our party at the Priory." He smiled reassuringly. "He has never been here before and we think he has wandered into the garden, or perhaps into this house by mistake."

"It sounds very . . . strange," Valencia said.

Then she saw that Sir Roger Crawford was staring at her in a manner that had nothing to do with their search, but because she was a woman.

Suddenly she became aware that she was only half-dressed and that her hair was flowing over her shoulders.

Because she felt embarrassed, she said quickly:

"As you can see, Sir, there is no one else in here, and you should certainly not have come into my bedroom when I had already retired!"

"You must excuse us," Edward Ward said, "but to make certain that is true, I am sure you will not mind my looking in your wardrobe."

Valencia drew herself up and said:

"I am astonished, Sir, whoever you may be, that you do not accept my word that there is no one here in this room except myself!"

Edward Ward paid her no attention.

He walked to the wardrobe, jerking it open to see nothing more incriminating than Valencia's gowns hanging up inside it.

He bent to look underneath the bed, but as he was doing so, Sir Roger went to Valencia's side.

"You must forgive us for upsetting you," he said

in a low voice, "but it is worrying when a friend has had too much to drink at dinner."

He smiled at her before going on:

"He might then go wandering about, perhaps endangering his life in the process."

His lips were saying one thing, but his eyes were roving over Valencia.

He took in the loveliness of her small, pointed face, and the soft curves of her body.

They were not concealed by the light negligee she was wearing.

Because she felt he was insulting her, she took a step backwards and, to her relief, Edward Ward said:

"There is no one here! Come on, Roger, we will have to look at the other rooms before we beard the Vicar in his den!"

He walked out as he spoke, but Sir Roger lingered.

"You are very beautiful!" he said in a low voice. "I want to see you again."

"I . . . I am afraid that is impossible!" Valencia said with her chin up. "And I consider it . . . extremely impertinent that you and your friend should come bursting into my . . . room in such an . . . extraordinary manner!"

"I will make my apologies tomorrow," Sir Roger said.

As he spoke there was a shout from the passage.

"Roger! Where are you?"

Sir Roger smiled at Valencia ingratiatingly before he hurried from the room, closing the door behind him.

She waited until they had gone.

Then quickly, twisting her long hair into a chignon and pinning it securely, she dressed herself once again in her muslin gown.

She waited for the searchers to leave the house.

They did not take long.

As she heard the front-door close she heard her father's voice say in a tone which made her know how angry he was:

"Good-night, Gentlemen, and I hope you find whom you are seeking!"

Now Valencia knew she must go back to the Earl and contrive in some way to bring him back to consciousness.

But she waited for her father to come up the stairs, blowing out the candles as he went.

He walked into his own bed-room.

She had the frightening feeling that what she was planning would not be as easy as she had anticipated.

chapter four

THE Earl opened his eyes and looked around him with surprise.

He realised he was not in the gilded carved canopied bed in which he had been sleeping at the Priory.

The plain white ceiling was very different from his own, painted by a Master Craftsman.

Then, as he moved his head to look sideways, someone rose from the window and came towards him.

"Are you awake?" a soft voice asked.

The Earl looked up to see two large blue eyes and what appeared to be a halo of golden hair.

The sun from the window made it somehow radiant, so that it seemed almost alive.

He stared at this vision for a few seconds before he managed to say with difficulty:

"Where . . . am . . . I?"

"You are quite safe," the soft voice replied. "Go to sleep and you will feel better in a few hours."

"I . . . am . . . thirsty."

"Of course you are."

She moved out of sight. Then he felt an arm raising him gently from the pillow and a glass being held to his lips.

He drank thirstily, aware that his mouth was very dry and his throat hurt him.

He thought what he drank was some sort of fruit-juice, but it was very sweet, and slipping down his throat took away the soreness.

Then he was lying back against the pillows again, and after a moment he said, his voice stronger:

"You have . . . not told me . . . where I . . . am."

The blue eyes were back looking down at him and she said:

"You had much better sleep, but in case you are worried, you are at your Chaplain's house, and no-one knows you are here. I promise that you are safe."

The Earl tried to remember what danger he had encountered, but failed.

Then because it was too much effort, he shut his eyes and knew no more.

When he woke again, realising he had slept for a long time, he heard the same soft voice say to someone else:

"It is quite all right, Nanny, I will look after His Lordship until one o'clock, then I will call you. Do go to bed and sleep."

"It is not right, Miss Valencia, that you should be in a gentleman's room."

There was a gentle laugh.

"It is too late to think of convention, Nanny. If I do not look after him, there is no-one else except you, and if you get over-tired, we shall all go hungry. Go to bed, and I promise I will call you at one o'clock."

The Earl heard what was obviously an older woman leave the room grumbling beneath her breath.

He was then aware that the girl with blue eyes, who he now knew was Valencia, was looking down at him again.

"You are awake," she said.

Now there was a lilt in her voice.

"I am . . . awake," he replied, "and I want to . . . know what is . . . happening."

"Do you think you are strong enough?"

"What has . . . happened to . . . me?"

He realised that she hesitated as if she were afraid to tell him the truth.

Then she said:

"You were drugged, and it is going to take a little while to get the poison out of your body."

"Drugged?"

"Yes, the port you drank last night at dinner was heavily drugged."

The Earl drew in his breath, then said:

"Suppose you tell . . . me exactly what has . . . happened. I feel I . . . must be . . . dreaming."

"I think it would be best if you waited until tomorrow morning."

"You know perfectly well," he replied, "that it would be . . . impossible for me to . . . do that. I should lie . . . awake wondering and . . . worrying, which I am sure . . . would be . . . bad for me."

Valencia gave a little laugh.

"Now you are blackmailing me! Very well, if you feel strong enough, I will tell you exactly what has occurred. First I think you would like something to drink."

She brought him the same concoction he had drunk before.

He knew as it slipped down his throat it not only took away the soreness, but made him feel better.

"What are you giving me?" he asked as she took the glass from his lips.

"Nothing more frightening than fruit, some herbs which my mother always said were antidotes for poison, and honey."

With a little effort the Earl pushed himself up on his pillows.

"Now," he said, and his voice was much stronger. "I want to know what is . . . happening."

He thought as he spoke that Valencia was very lovely.

He was astonished at finding anything so beautiful in his Chaplain's house, although why he was there he had no idea.

Valencia set the glass down on a table.

When she came back she looked at the chair beside the bed.

Then, realising she would be lower than the Earl, seated herself without being in the least self-conscious on the mattress facing him.

It was a large bed, and now that he was sitting up, the Earl could see that the room in which he had been sleeping was very attractive.

Although he was shrewd enough to realise there was nothing expensive or luxurious about it.

The curtains over the window were a pretty colour and so were the walls.

The bed had muslin curtains hanging on each side of it.

Then he looked again at Valencia and thought he had not been mistaken in thinking she was very lovely.

He saw she was wearing a warm dressing gown of thin blue wool.

It had narrow lace around the small collar, and lace at the edge of the sleeves.

When he looked at her eyes he knew she was regarding him anxiously.

She was considering whether to hear the truth would be too much for him.

"I am better, much better," he said as if he read her thoughts, "and I therefore want to know . . . why I am here and why . . . as you said . . . I have been drugged. . . ."

Slowly and a little shyly, Valencia told him what she had overheard in the Chapel.

What she had done after deciding to save him from being married and her father from being threatened if he did not agree to co-operate.

"So you put me in a Priests' Hole," the Earl said. "I had no idea there was . . . anything so interesting and in this case . . . so useful in the Chapel."

"Fortunately no-one else knew about it," Valencia said.

"When I am well enough, I should like to see it. I

am also curious to know how you got me out, as you said you had to climb down a ladder to get into it."

Valencia gave a little laugh, which was what he had heard when he first became conscious.

"It was difficult," she said, "and only possible because Ben is so strong. He carried you over his shoulder as he climbed up the ladder, then I pulled you onto the flagged floor until he could pick you up again."

"It seems incredible," the Earl remarked, "but go on."

"We brought you back here down the underground passage, and as I knew Mr. Ward and Sir Roger had already searched the house, I thought it unlikely that they would do so again."

She paused, gave a little laugh, and then went on:

"In fact, no-one had come near us today, but Ben tells me they have been scouring the grounds and there is talk of getting someone to drag the lake to see if you are there."

The Earl laughed.

"I see that I constitute somewhat of a problem! At the time it is difficult to know how to—thank you for—saving me."

"I am glad I was able to do so."

Now, because the Earl was looking at her, Valencia felt shy.

She would have moved off the bed had he not put out his hand to cover hers.

"I am very, very grateful," he said, "because I have no intention of marrying Lady Hester or anyone else."

He felt her fingers quiver beneath his, and as if he could read her thoughts, he added:

"I realise that one day I shall require an heir for the Priory, but there is no hurry, and I certainly have no intention of being drugged into matrimony."

There was now a note of anger in his voice.

When he finished speaking, his mouth was set in a hard line.

He could remember how his father had always said all women were treacherous, deceitful, and dangerous. He had been right, completely and absolutely right.

He took his hand away from Valencia's.

He told himself he hated the whole sex and everything about them.

Then, as he stared with unseeing eyes across the bed-room, he heard a tremulous voice say:

"Please do not let this . . . spoil you. If you become . . . hard and . . . cynical, it will spoil your happiness as well as the . . . happiness of so many people who rely on you."

The Earl stared at her in astonishment before he said:

"What do you expect me to feel in the circumstances? Except that I have made a fool of myself, and should not have trusted anyone in the first place."

There had been a distinct pause when he had obviously been about to say "a woman."

Then he realised Valencia was one and changed it.

But Valencia knew what he had been about to say.

As she got off the bed he felt he had hurt her.

"Of course," he said, "everyone is not the same,

81

but perhaps in my new position this is what I must be prepared to expect."

"Of course you must not expect anything of the sort!" Valencia replied quickly. "Because you are the Earl of Dolphinston, people will admire you and naturally there will be a few who envy you."

She paused a moment.

"But I can't believe that all your friends are equally wicked and capable of doing such terrible things as you have just suffered."

The Earl did not speak, and after a moment she went on:

"If you suspect everyone you meet, and are suspicious of those who really want to be friends, then you will spoil the beauty and happiness of the Priory, and although you may not realise it . . . be miserable yourself. . . . "

There was a faint twist to the Earl's lips as he said:

"I think, Miss Hadley, you are preaching at me!"

Valencia gave a little cry.

"I did not mean to do so. Forgive me if it sounded impertinent. Yet because I love the Priory and it means so much to everyone who lives here, I want you to . . . love it, too, and to be . . . everything we expect the Earl of Dolphinston to . . . be."

"And what do you expect?" the Earl enquired.

Standing by his bed, Valencia did not look at him but over his head as she said:

"I expect you to be very . . . dignified because of your importance, at the same time . . . kind, understanding, and above all things . . . just."

She drew in her breath before she went on:

"I expect you also to set an example, as you have done . . . already by your bravery . . . to all those who serve you and who . . . look up to you. Because they will be proud of you, they will try to . . . emulate you and be . . . like you."

Her voice died away, and the Earl said:

"I understand what you are saying to me, and I think you are asking rather a lot of a mere soldier."

Valencia shook her head.

"You are not a mere soldier now. You have taken the place of . . . someone we all loved. Although it seems cruel and . . . unnecessary that George and William should both have . . . died."

There was a little sob in her voice before she added:

"I feel sure you are the . . . right person to . . . follow the last Earl, and that is what I want . . . everyone else . . . to feel."

She spoke with a sincerity which even though she spoke very quietly seemed to vibrate towards him.

After a moment the Earl said:

"Thank you, but I feel you are asking too much."

He shut his eyes as he spoke, and in a moment Valencia's attitude turned to one of concern.

"You are tired," she said. "Please lie down again and go to sleep. If you do not do so, you will not feel well and strong in the morning, and remember, there are a great . . . many things you . . . have to do . . . now you have come . . . home."

There was a faint smile on the Earl's lips as he said sleepily:

"I am quite certain you are . . . ready to tell me what they . . . are."

                    *   *   *

Valencia was arranging flowers in the Sitting-Room,
when the door opened and someone came into the
room.

She stood back from the large vase of white lilac
she had arranged on a table near the mantelpiece.

She said as she did so:

"They smell lovely, Nanny."

There was no answer and she turned her head,
then gave a little exclamation of surprise.

It was not Nanny who had come into the room as
she had thought, but Sir Roger Crawford. He was
elegantly dressed in riding-breeches and a cut-away
coat.

But the expression in his eyes as he walked towards her made her heart give a little leap of fear.

"I was not . . . expecting . . . you," she said nervously. "Why . . . are you . . . here?"

"I told you I wanted to see you again," Sir Roger
replied, "but unfortunately, owing to the search for
the missing Earl, I was unable to come yesterday."

"I am . . . afraid I am . . . very busy," Valencia said
hastily.

"Not too busy for me," he answered. "I want to
talk to you, and I want you to tell me why, when
you are so beautiful, you hide yourself in this God-
forsaken hole."

Valencia stiffened, and he went on:

"Surely you realise you would be a sensation in
London, and that is where I would like to take you."

He was standing in front of her as he spoke.

His eyes seemed to be devouring her, so that instinctively she took a step away from him.

"My father is in . . . his Study," she said nervously. "And I am sure he would . . . like to . . . meet you."

"I have no wish to meet your father or anyone else," Sir Roger said. "It is you I want to talk to, so stop running away, Valencia, and listen to what I have to say."

She moved farther away from him, but he reached out his hand and caught her by the wrist.

"You are lovely; ridiculously, absurdly lovely," he exclaimed, "and I can think of better things we might do than waste our time talking."

His arm began to encircle her.

Because she realised that he was drawing her closer to him, she gave a cry of fear and started to struggle.

"I want to kiss you!" Sir Roger said. "And I suspect you have not been kissed before. I can assure you, Valencia, you will find it very delightful, as I shall."

"Leave me . . . alone!" Valencia cried. "Please . . . leave me alone!"

She fought frantically against him, but realised he was very strong.

He was pulling her nearer and nearer to him.

There was what seemed to her a fire in his eyes, also an expression on his face which told her he was amused by her resistance.

He was also confident that however hard she fought him, he would eventually be the conqueror.

"Let . . . me go! Let . . . me go!" she pleaded.

As his arms went around her, she turned her head from side to side to avoid his lips.

It was then the door opened, and to Valencia's utter relief, Nanny came into the room.

As she did so, Sir Roger loosened his hold and then Valencia pulled herself free and ran across the room.

She passed Nanny without speaking, running through the small hall and up the stairs.

Without really thinking, she opened the door to the spare-room, where the Earl was still lying in bed.

He was reading the newspapers.

She came in, closed the door behind her, and leant against it, breathing quickly from the speed at which she had run.

He stared at her in surprise.

"What has happened? What has upset you?" he enquired.

"It is . . . Sir Roger," Valencia gasped, "but it is . . . all right, he does not know . . . you are here, he came . . . to see me."

"Came to see you?" the Earl asked. "Why should he do that?"

Valencia did not answer, and he said:

"I realise that was a stupid question. The point is, you are to have nothing whatever to do with him."

"I have . . . no wish . . . to," Valencia murmured.

As she spoke, she sat down in the chair as if her legs could not carry her any farther, and added:

"I . . . hate him! He is . . . horrible!"

"I presume he tried to kiss you," the Earl remarked.

"How could he...dare to...do such a...
thing?" Valencia demanded.

She did not say any more.

It was obvious from the expression on her face
how much she was upset by what had occurred.

"Forget him!" the Earl said sharply. "There is no
reason for you to see him again."

"He may...call," Valencia whispered, "and he
frightened...me."

"I am going to get up," the Earl said suddenly.
"Please send Ben to help me."

"It is too...soon!" Valencia exclaimed. "I know
you still feel...weak from the drug they...gave
you and Mama always said if someone was poisoned
...it took a...long time to clear from...their sys-
tem."

"I am strong enough to do what I intend to do,"
the Earl said, "and that is to chase those people out
of my house!"

There was a determined note in his voice which
made Valencia forget about herself.

She rose from the chair in which she had sat
down.

"What I want you to do," the Earl went on, "is to
send someone to my Stables with this letter, which is
to be carried to London by one of the grooms immediately."

He paused and then continued:

"It is to my secretary, who will have returned
there, telling him that Lady Hester and her brother
are no longer my guests in Park Lane and he is to
make that clear to them when they return."

"When they return," Valencia repeated slowly, "but . . . supposing they do not . . . leave here?"

"They will go when I tell them to," the Earl said.

She went nearer to the bed.

"But they may try again to make you . . . marry Lady Hester? They can . . . threaten you or perhaps use more . . . violent means to make you . . . marry her."

"I think they are unlikely to do that," the Earl said lightly. "Now that I am on my guard, I promise you, Valencia, I will not drink anything they give me or eat anything that can be tampered with."

He saw she was not convinced, and went on:

"I know you will agree that if I am to take my place in the proper manner as the Earl of Dolphinston, I must first clear the decks of people whom I cannot trust, and who should not have come here with me in the first place."

"Of course I want . . . you to do . . . that," Valencia said, "but you must be . . . careful. I am afraid . . . terribly . . . afraid that they will . . . trick you in . . . some way."

"Does it really matter so much to you?" the Earl asked.

She thought there was a mocking note in his voice that had not been there before.

"It matters to . . . everyone who lives on your Estate, and to whom the . . . Priory means so . . . much."

There was a little silence.

Then, as if she had to say what was in her mind, she went on:

"The farmers are hurt because you have not called on them, and the game-keepers, the gardeners, the carpenters, the woodcutters, and, of course, the pensioners in the village are all . . . longing to . . . meet you."

She looked at him a little nervously, and the Earl said ruefully:

"You are making me realise that I have got off on the wrong foot. Very well, let me get up so that I can start to put things right, and I promise you I will be in no danger."

"If you feel it is too much . . . you will go back to bed?" Valencia asked.

"I promise," the Earl replied.

He gave her a flashing smile as she went to the door of his room.

"I will find Ben," she said, "but you must remember he is better with horses than with human beings."

The Earl laughed.

Then he heard her stop outside and knew she was making sure that Sir Roger had left the house before she went downstairs.

In fact, Nanny had shown him out.

She had done so without speaking, in a manner which had made him feel as if he were back in the Nursery and certainly in disgrace.

He sprang into the saddle of his horse waiting outside, which he had ordered Ben to look after.

Then, as he rode towards the Priory, he looked back and saw Valencia standing at the front-door talking to Ben.

He told himself that for the moment he was defeated but he would certainly insist upon seeing her again.

He was just about to ride on, when an idea came to him.

He moved through the trees which surrounded the Chaplain's House and, out of sight of the front-door, found his way to the kitchen entrance.

He did not dismount, but sat looking at the door which was ajar.

Almost as if he had called her, a maid-servant came outside.

She tipped a bucket containing the peelings from potatoes into a bin, which would be later taken to the pig-sties at the Home Farm.

As she emptied the pail, Emily looked in surprise at the smart gentleman on horseback.

"I wonder if you can help me?" Sir Roger asked.

Emily put down the pail and moved towards him.

"I can see you are a clever girl," he said, "and I have been wondering if, by any chance, you have seen any sign of the lost Earl. I have been looking for him everywhere, and I have a golden guinea in my pocket for anyone who is able to tell me where he is likely to be."

As he spoke, he took a guinea from the pocket of his waist-coat and held it out in his hand so that it glittered in the sunshine.

Emily looked at it, fascinated. Then she said:

"Oi've bin told t'tell no one nothin' as to who's in the house, Sir."

Sir Roger's eyes narrowed.

"And who told you to say nothing?" he asked.

"Miss Valencia tol' me t'say nothin', Sir, so there's nothin' Oi can say."

"No, of course not," Sir Roger agreed, putting the golden guinea back into his pocket.

Then with a smile on his lips he rode quickly towards the Priory.

*　*　*

Valencia was in the Study, when she heard somebody on the stairs.

She went from the room to see the Earl coming down carefully, holding on to the bannisters.

She started across the hall towards him.

"Do be careful!" she begged. "I am sure it is much too soon!"

"You are molly-coddling me!" he said. "As a matter of fact, I feel so much better, and I cannot go on playing the invalid just to please you and Nanny."

Valencia laughed.

"You may well laugh," the Earl said, "but I have been given strict instructions as to what I may do or may not do! And, of course, I dare not disobey her!"

Valencia laughed again.

"We all have to obey Nanny," she said, "and you will be no exception."

"Where is your father?"

"He is in the Study," Valencia replied. "He will be thrilled that you are so much better. At the same time, he finds it hard to come back to anything as mundane as the modern world when he is lost in the excitements of Ancient Greece."

They had reached the Study by this time and Valencia opened the door.

"Our guest is better, Papa," she said.

There was a little pause before the Vicar looked

up from the book he was reading as he sat at his desk.

Then, as he saw the Earl, he rose to his feet.

"Good-morning, My Lord! I am glad to see you recovered."

"Thanks entirely to your daughter and to your Nurse," the Earl said, "and, of course, I am extremely grateful for your hospitality."

"I am only glad that Valencia was able to save you," the Vicar said.

The Earl sat down in a high-backed chair.

"I want to talk to you about a great number of things, but first of all I want you to help me to get to know my people."

He paused and then continued:

"I suggest that you introduce me to the farmers in their correct order of precedence, and later Valencia has a whole list of people on whom I should have called before now."

He glanced somewhat critically at Valencia as he spoke.

She was looking at him, thinking as she did so that now that he was dressed he looked very different from the man whom she had been tending as an invalid.

It was true that the clothes he was wearing, which were what he had borrowed yesterday from the Vicar, were not as smart as what he would normally have worn.

But he seemed to have an authority and a consequence. It made him very different from the man who had lain weakly in bed.

She had ministered to him in the same way as she would have cared for a sick child.

Now she knew he was the best-looking man she had ever seen.

At the same time, he seemed completely separated from her because he was so self-sufficient.

It was impossible to think that having such a strong personality and authoritative manner he could ever be influenced or even hurt by anyone.

She knew, of course, that it was what he should be as the Earl of Dolphinston.

She was sure that once he was rid of the people who had tried to trick him into marriage, he would be everything that was expected in the heart of the family.

"Now, what I am going to suggest . . ." the Earl began.

Even as he spoke, the door of the Study was flung open.

As Valencia gave a cry of horror, Edward Ward walked into the room with his sister, Lady Hester.

She was looking even more beautiful and elegantly gowned than when Valencia had first seen her.

She was wearing a gown of emerald green that matched the feathers that fluttered in her high-crowned bonnet and the emeralds that glittered round her neck.

There were also emerald bracelets on each of her wrists.

Her eyes had a sudden light in them as she saw the Earl.

She ran across the room to throw herself on her knees beside the chair in which he was sitting.

Then she said in a voice redolent with emotion:

"Darling, we have found you! How could you have frightened us all so terribly by disappearing in that strange manner?"

The Earl pushed away Lady Hester's hands, which tried to cling to him.

He rose slowly to his feet, and as he towered above her, he said:

"I have learned exactly what happened the night before last, so I do not think you will be surprised when I ask you to leave my house immediately, for I have no wish to see any of you again!"

Lady Hester gave a cry of protest as she rose from the floor.

"How can you say anything so cruel, so wicked?" she answered. "I love you, Hue, and you know how happy we have been together."

She moved towards him again but the Earl put her to one side.

"I mean what I say!" he said firmly.

"If that is your last word," Edward Ward replied, "then it is time I had something to say and it is quite simple—I have no intention, Dolphinston, of allowing you to treat my sister in such an outrageous fashion."

Edward took a step towards the Earl and continued:

"You made it very clear what you felt about her and, as you know, she loves you. You will, therefore, do the right thing and marry her."

"And if I refuse?" the Earl asked.

"If you refuse, I shall have to take stronger measures to persuade you to behave like a gentleman."

As he spoke, he drew a revolver from the pocket of his coat and pointed it at the Earl.

There was a moment's silence. Then the Earl said:

"If you intend to shoot me, I cannot imagine I shall be much use as a bridegroom."

"I have no intention of killing you," Edward Ward answered, "but unless you marry my sister, I shall certainly wound you and also your Chaplain, unless he performs the wedding, for which we have a Special Licence."

His voice became a snarl as he added:

"I assure you I am not speaking lightly. You will marry Hester or you will rue the consequences, and find it very painful to do so."

There was silence after he had spoken, and it seemed to Valencia as if everybody were waiting for the Earl's response.

Edward Ward was pointing his revolver at the Earl's shoulder, where she guessed he intented to wound him.

Lady Hester was standing beside the Earl with a faint smile on her red lips, as if she knew he had no way of defending himself.

Sir Roger was just inside the door.

He was looking, as Valencia knew, at her rather than at the drama that was taking place.

The Vicar, seemingly stunned into silence, was behind his desk and, therefore, quite incapable, Valencia thought, of helping the Earl.

Then, as if she could read the Earl's thoughts as she had been able to read them when he was sick, she was aware what he was wondering.

It was, if he struck Edward Ward, he would be able to pull the trigger before the blow landed.

'What can I do? What can he do?' Valencia wondered.

It was then she saw amongst a number of other things lying on her father's desk, an open box containing pins.

They were there to pin together the pages of his translation, to prevent them from being blown away.

Almost without thinking she picked a pin up in her hand, and as she did so, she knew what she must do.

She was standing just behind Lady Hester.

Making a movement which no one could see because all eyes were on the Earl, she stuck the pin as hard as she could into Lady Hester's naked arm.

Lady Hester uttered a shrill scream of pain.

Inevitably her brother turned his head to see what was wrong.

As he did so, the Earl punched him with an upper-cut on the chin.

It all happened in the flash of a second, and as Edward Ward fell backwards onto the floor, his revolver clattered from his hand. The Earl bent to pick it up.

He then took control, and although he did not raise his voice, it seemed to echo round the walls as he said:

"I want you all out of this room and out of my house, and if you have not left within an hour, I will have you thrown out by the servants. Is that clear?"

Now his pistol was pointed at Sir Roger, who had walked to where Edward Ward was lying.

The Earl's upper-cut had knocked him out and he had been, for the moment, unconscious.

But he was now opening his eyes and trying to move his mouth, which was extremely painful.

Sir Roger helped him stagger to his feet, and without saying anything more, led him towards the door.

Lady Hester, holding her arm, made one last effort.

"Hue," she said, and her voice was low and soft, "I am sure you and I can talk about this . . ."

"You will leave with your brother!" the Earl said.

It was a command.

His eyes were hard and Lady Hester was too worldly-wise not to know when a man had no feeling for her except one of utter contempt.

For a moment she defied him.

"I hate you, Hue! Do you hear that? I hate you and I shall do my best to hurt you in the same way that you have hurt me!"

The Earl did not speak and for one moment she hesitated, hoping to see some weakening, some softening in his eyes.

He obviously was waiting for her to go.

Her brother, supported by Sir Roger, had nearly reached the front-door.

She swept from the room, her head high, her emeralds glinting.

The manner of her exit was obviously intended to indicate that she was not defeated and that in some way she would avenge herself.

It was impossible for anybody in the room to

move until she had passed through the door and was out of sight.

Then Valencia crossed the room and closed the door of the Study.

As she did so, the Earl sat down in a chair by the Vicar's desk and closed his eyes.

"It has been too much for him," the Vicar said.

He went to a cabinet, opened the door, and took out a small bottle of brandy to pour some into a glass.

He handed it to the Earl, who drank it without argument.

They saw the color come back into his face.

Valencia realised that her father was looking at her ruminatively, and she said:

"I will go and see if luncheon is ready and, afterwards, I think His Lordship should go back to bed."

She did not wait for a reply but hurried across to the kitchen.

As she crossed the hall she could see that the carriage which had brought Lady Hester, her brother, and Sir Roger was already disappearing down the short drive.

"I have . . . saved him . . . and for the . . . second time!" she told herself.

Then, almost as if a voice told her so, she knew that Lady Hester would try again.

The Earl was not yet out of the wood.

chapter five

"THEY were thrilled to meet you," Valencia said.

They were leaving the third of the farms which the Earl had inspected.

She was glad that he appeared very much at home with the simple people who worked on the Dolphin Estate, as their forebears had done for many generations.

He admired their live-stock, accepted a glass of home-made cider, and complimented the farmer's wife on the attractiveness of the house.

Everybody seemed so pleased with the Earl's attention.

Valencia felt a little thrill of happiness because she knew she had made him aware of his responsibilities.

It was also an inexpressible joy that he had disposed of Lady Hester and the two men who had come with her.

She had been terribly afraid they would not leave the Priory.

But she learnt later in the day, after the Earl had returned home, that they had obeyed his instructions.

They had left within an hour of the scene that had been enacted in her father's Study.

"I wish I could be sure," she said to the Vicar, "that they will now leave the Earl alone and not try any more wicked tricks."

"I am both surprised and horrified," her father said quietly, "and I hope the Earl will have learnt from this experience that 'one cannot touch pitch without being defiled.'"

Valencia, however, was prepared to lay the whole blame on Lady Hester for what had happened.

She felt the dark-eyed beauty was as sensuous as a snake and as poisonous.

Because her father was so eager to get on with his book, he had left it to her to take the Earl round the estate.

She had been only too willing to comply.

She wanted more than anything else to see the reaction of the people to their new Master.

Also, to make sure that the Earl understood how much the Priory, and, above all, he himself meant to them.

In between visiting the farms, which were some distance apart from each other, they called on several cottagers and inspected a School.

Valencia also showed him another small but beautiful Norman Church which was on the far North of his estate.

There was no incumbent at the moment, and her

father therefore took the Serivces there every other week.

The Vicarage was shut and the blinds drawn over the windows, and almost without thinking Valencia said:

"It would be lovely if you appointed a young Vicar here who could not only take the Services, but also organise Cricket and Football matches with the other villages."

"Are you suggesting that also comes under my jurisdiction?" the Earl asked in surprise.

"Of course," Valencia replied, "you choose the Vicar, you pay his stipend, and you can instruct him as to what other duties you wish him to perform besides those of arranging the Services."

"I think there should be a hand-book for Landlords!" the Earl said ruefully. Valencia laughed.

"There will be plenty of people to tell you what is expected without your needing a hand-book!"

"You are my chief instructress," the Earl said, "and I am relying on you not to let me make any mistakes or fail in my duties."

He was speaking half-seriously, half-mockingly, and Valencia wondered if he resented a woman telling him these things and would have preferred to hear them from her father.

At the same time, she could not help feeling that she could make his new duties more understandable even than her father could have done.

It was late when they returned home.

As the Earl drew his horses to a standstill outside the Chaplain's House, he said:

"I would like to see your father, if he is available."

"He will be in the Study," Valencia replied, "and he will not have the slightest idea that we have been gone for so long."

She laughed as she spoke.

The Earl, however, looked serious, and she wondered what he was thinking.

They went into the Study.

As Valencia expected, her father came back reluctantly to reality from the world in which he was immersed. He rose to greet the Earl.

She would have gone from the room, but the Earl said quickly:

"Do not go, Valencia! What I have to say to your father concerns you."

"Concerns me?" Valencia questioned.

She was thinking perhaps she had done something wrong.

"Would you like some refreshment?" the Vicar asked as the Earl seated himself in an arm-chair beside the fireplace.

The Earl shook his head.

"I shall be going back to the Priory as soon as we have had a little talk, and I know Mrs. Brooke will be planning a large dinner for me. She is so insistent that I need 'feeding up' that I am half-afraid I shall soon be too heavy for my horses!"

The Vicar laughed, but Valencia said:

"I am sure that will not happen! In any case your horses needed the exercise you have been giving them since you arrived."

"I understand from my grooms," the Earl replied,

"that you took my place very adequately when I was not here."

She looked at him a little anxiously.

She was wondering if he was annoyed. In the months between the last Earl's death and his coming home she had every day ridden the horses that filled the stables with nothing to do.

As if he could read her thoughts, he said:

"I am not complaining, merely pointing out that you were aware of what was required, while I was in London!"

Valencia gave a little sigh of relief.

Then as the Vicar sat down in another chair, the Earl said:

"I have been wondering how I can reward Valencia for saving me so courageously, and—"

Before he could say any more, Valencia gave a cry and exclaimed:

"But . . . of course . . . I do not want any reward! Please . . . do not think of anything so foolish!"

The Earl ignored her and, looking at her father, went on:

"I suppose in the normal course of events a diamond necklace, or a jewelled brooch, would be considered a proper present, but I do not feel at the moment that Valencia has much opportunity of wearing such trinkets."

Valencia laughed.

"That is certainly true! Of course the horses would admire me, but I cannot help thinking I should feel over-dressed!"

The Earl did not join in her laughter but said to the Vicar:

"What I am going to suggest, and I hope it will meet with your approval, is that Valencia should go to London and stay for a month or so with my maternal grandmother, the Duchess of Wakefield."

He saw Valencia's eyes widen in astonishment and went on:

"I have seen her several times since I returned from abroad, and although she is getting on in years, she is still very active and extremely social."

He stopped speaking to smile at her before he went on:

"I am sure she would enjoy having Valencia with her, and I can think of nobody better to present her to the Queen at Windsor or, in her absence, to the Prince of Wales and Princess Alexandra."

As he finished speaking there was a moment of stunned silence.

Then Valencia said quickly:

"It is . . . very kind of you to . . . think of me, but of course I could not . . . possibly do . . . anything like that! It would all be far . . . too grand for . . . me."

The Earl did not look at her, but at the Vicar, and he said quietly:

"Now I have learnt that Valencia's mother was a Dolphin and I know quite well she would want and expect her daughter to enjoy the sort of life I am offering her."

"When you put it like that, My Lord," the Vicar replied, "it is difficult for me not to agree!"

Valencia jumped to her feet.

"But of course you cannot agree, Papa! How can I possibly go to London looking as I do? You know as well as I do that it would be impossible for us to afford the very many expensive clothes I should need."

"When my grandmother hears of how you saved my life and looked after me, I know she will be only too willing to provide you with any clothes you need," the Earl remarked.

He paused before he continued:

"Not only to make your curtsy in a 'Drawing-Room,' also at the parties, Balls, and Receptions to which you will be invited and to which she will chaperon you."

"It is really very kind of you to think of it," the Vicar said after a moment's pause, "but, of course, it is a decision which must rest with my daughter."

He was about to say more, when Nanny opened the door to say:

"Mrs. Higgins here to see you, Sir, about the choir on Sunday. Says she's got an appointment."

"Yes, yes, of course," the Vicar replied. "I told her to call on me this evening."

He rose, saying as he did so:

"I hope, My Lord, you will excuse me, and perhaps you will discuss your suggestion with Valencia."

He went from the Study, and Valencia said:

"As Papa has said, it is very kind of you, but you do understand it is something I cannot do?"

"That is a ridiculous assertion!" the Earl replied. "It is something I intend you shall do—in fact, I insist on it!"

He saw the expression on Valencia's face and went on:

"Good heavens, child! You must realise you are

wasted here, seeing nobody and spending your life looking after my people and riding my horses."

There was a scathing note in his voice which made Valencia say quickly:

"That is . . . all I . . . want to do, and I am . . . very happy."

"You only think you are because you have known nothing else, and therefore I intend, whatever you may say about it, to take you to London with me tomorrow to stay with my grandmother."

He paused before he went on. "If after a few weeks you hate it as much as you think you will, then, of course, you may come back."

"Are you . . . ordering me to . . . obey you?"

"I prefer to ask you to do what I want," the Earl replied, "but if you do not, then I shall, of course, make it a command!"

He spoke lightly, but she saw the determination on his face.

Petulantly she walked away to stand looking down into the fireplace.

"I cannot think why you want to . . . upset everything," she said after a moment. "As I have told you I . . . am perfectly . . . happy as I am."

"You told me to take over my responsibilities," the Earl said, "and as you are definitely one of them, you must allow me to believe that I know what is best for you."

There was a note of determination as hard as steel in his voice.

Valencia felt it would be no use to go on arguing with him.

"Very well!" she said. "As you are determined to

have your own way, I can only say that if I disappoint you or embarrass you by not knowing how to behave, you must not blame me!"

The Earl rose from his chair.

"Now that that is settled, I will go back to the Priory. I would like you to be ready to leave by nine o'clock tomorrow morning."

"Why have you suddenly decided to go back to London?" Valencia asked. "I thought you were . . . happy here!"

"I am," the Earl replied, "but I have received a letter from the Comptroller to the Prince of Wales saying that His Royal Highness wishes me to accompany him to a Regimental Banquet and it is something I cannot refuse."

He knew, without Valencia saying so, that she was frightened that once he returned to London, Lady Hester would be waiting for him and perhaps try to trap him.

She did not say what she was thinking, but it vibrated towards the Earl, and he said:

"Forget her! Everything that happened is now a closed chapter, and I do not want you to think or speak of it again."

He walked from the Study as he spoke.

Valencia followed him into the hall.

He picked up his hat, which was lying on the chair where he had left it. As he did so, he realised she was looking at him with an expression on her face that was half one of pleading, half of fear.

"I want you to enjoy yourself, Valencia," he said, "and I promise you my grandmother will look after you, and so will I. When you are tired of London, you can always come back to the country, and all I am asking is that you give it a fair trial."

"I . . . I cannot think why. . . ." Valencia began.

But already he had reached the front-door and passed through it to where his horse was waiting.

Then, as Valencia stood in the doorway looking very forlorn, he raised his hat to her and rode away.

"He is being very high-handed and interfering!" Valencia said to herself. "I wish he would leave me alone!"

But she knew, if she were honest, that that was not entirely true.

* * *

Nevertheless, when the next morning came, Valencia drove away with the Earl in a travelling-carriage drawn by four horses.

As they did so, she could not help a little wave of excitement moving through her.

"Now, you enjoy yourself," Nanny said as she helped her to dress, "and don't go worrying your head about your father."

She paused a moment and then went on:

"You know as well as I do he'll be lost in his books. I'll remind him about Services and see he don't forget anything more than usual until you come back."

"I shall be home-sick, Nanny," Valencia said, "and also afraid of doing the wrong thing without Mama to guide me."

"It's everything your mother'd have wanted for you," Nanny said. "She used to say to me some-times: 'This'll be a dull life for Valencia when she grows up, with so little happening in the country, and we can't afford to entertain as I'd like so that people'll be obliged to ask us back."

"If Mama were alive . . . it would be different," Valencia complained. But Nanny would not listen.

As they drove off, she could not help thinking how handsome and well-dressed the Earl was.

She felt, in comparison, very much a country bumpkin.

She, however, forgot about herself during the drive, and when they finally reached London late in the afternoon, she was tired.

The Duchess of Wakefield, who had been notified of their arrival by the Earl, was waiting for them in her large and important house in Belgrave Square.

Although she was well over sixty, she still had a slim figure.

She was very elegantly dressed with her grey hair beautifully coiffured.

She held out both her hands to her grandson when he appeared.

"This is a delightful surprise, Hue!" she said. "I was afraid that you were enjoying life so much in the country that you had forgotten us all in London."

"But now I am back, Grandmama," the Earl said, "and I have brought my Chaplain's daughter with me, Valencia Hadley who, as I told you in my note, has rendered me a very great service for which I am eternally in her debt."

The Duchess looked curious, but she welcomed Valencia with an unmistakable sincerity, saying:

"How pretty you are, child, and very like your mother. Of course we must do everything to make you one of the most important debutantes of the Season."

Valencia gave a little cry.

"Oh . . . please . . . Ma'am," she said, "I have no wish to be that! In fact, I know I am going to feel like a 'fish out of water' and you will soon send me back to the country in . . . disgrace!"

The Duchess laughed.

"That is very unlikely! And you must be aware that my grandson's reputation of winning battles and gaining every possible award would be tarnished if that happened!"

"Now you are make *me* embarrassed!" the Earl complained.

They talked for a little while, then he said:

"I am going to leave Valencia with you, Grandmama, and as I have a great deal to do tomorrow and also am invited to a Banquet with the Prince that evening, I will call on you the day after."

Looking towards Valencia, he continued:

"I expect, in the meantime, you will have some shopping to occupy you both."

"That is an undeniable truth," the Duchess replied, "but you know we shall be awaiting your approval of our purchases, so do not forget us for too long."

The Earl kissed his grandmother's cheek, then as he took Valencia's hands in his she said in a low voice:

"You will . . . take care?"

"Stop worrying about me and think of yourself!" he ordered. "That is why I have brought you to London."

She wanted to tell him that it would be impossible for her not to worry about him.

He was back in what she thought of as "Lady Hester's own territory."

It was something that she could not put into words.

All too quickly she found herself alone with the Duchess.

"Now, the first thing you must tell me," she said, "is what you have done to make Hue so indebted to you! As you can imagine, I am extremely curious!"

"I think it is . . . something he should . . . tell you himself," Valencia faltered.

"As he has omitted to do so, I shall be very hurt if you do not confide in me," the Duchess said.

As she spoke beguilingly, with a sweetness that reminded Valencia of her own mother, she related exactly what had occurred from the moment the Earl had returned to the Priory, and she overheard Lady Hester, her brother, and Sir Roger plotting in the Chapel.

When she had finished, the Duchess drew in her breath and exclaimed:

"I can hardly believe that what you are telling me has not come out of some novelette!"

She shook her head as she continued:

"I have never heard of anything so disgraceful as Lady Hester's behaviour, but then, I always did think she was a fast woman and not at all the type of wife I have envisaged for my grandson."

"She is . . . very . . . beautiful."

"I am sure your Nanny, who my grandson said helped you to look after him, says, 'Beauty is only skin deep!' It is what my Nurse used to say when I was first a pretty little girl and then a beautiful debutante."

"I am sure you were lovely, Ma'am!"

She spoke sincerely, for the Duchess's classical features were still there.

She could visualise clearly how lovely she must have been when she was young.

"And when I have finished dressing you, you are going to be as beautiful, my dear," the Duchess was saying. "In fact, you must forgive me for saying so, but your gown is very old-fashioned and so is your travelling bonnet."

Valencia laughed.

"There is no one in the country to notice what I am wearing, except for the villagers, who think this is the height of fashion because they have nothing with which to compare it!"

"Perhaps that is a good thing!" the Duchess remarked, and they both laughed.

*   *   *

The next day, however, when Valencia and the Duchess went shopping, she realised that clothes were not a laughing matter.

They had to be considered very seriously.

Everything she saw in the shops on Bond Street into which the Duchess took her seemed more beautiful than the last.

But the Duchess rejected one thing after another, saying they were either too fussy, too plain, too old, or too young.

However, by luncheon-time Valencia possessed six new gowns with the promise of a dozen others.

She knew when she returned to Belgrave Square that she looked very different from the "country bumpkin" she had been when she arrived the day before.

But it was disappointing that the Earl was not there to admire her.

She thought that while at the Regimental Banquet he would hardly be likely even to give her a thought.

*   *   *

The next day proved even more disappointing.

He did not come to the large luncheon-party that the Duchess gave to introduce Valencia to her friends.

Nor to a Reception they attended in the afternoon.

Here she was introduced to so many people that she could not remember their names.

On their arrival home it was to find there was a message from the Earl.

It said that he was unavoidably prevented from coming to dinner as he had promised.

He hoped, however, it would be possible for him to join them at the Ball which he knew they were attending that night.

"A Ball?" Valencia exclaimed when the Duchess gave her the note. "You did not tell me we were going to a Ball!"

"I wanted to surprise you," the Duchess answered, "and I think you will enjoy it because it is being given by an old friend of mine to celebrate the birthday of her granddaughter who is about the same age as you are."

She smiled as she added:

"We do not have to go far—just to the other side of the Square, and I promised a long time ago to give a dinner-party for the Ball. It is extremely disappointing that Hue will not be with us!"

Valencia was dressed in a gown which made her look quite different in every way from how she had ever looked before.

She wished that the Earl could see her, if only for a few minutes.

Then it suddenly struck her that perhaps the reason that he was busy was that he was with Lady Hester again.

Valencia was quite certain she would not allow him to escape her a second time.

She would somehow contrive to inveigle him away, or cling to him at parties so that without making a scene he could not free himself.

Because she was worried about the Earl, it was difficult to concentrate on the compliments she was paid at the dinner-party.

Even less when she was dancing with the young men who were introduced to her during the course of the evening either by her hostess or else by the Duchess.

Incredible though it seemed, Valencia found them boring.

Although they were good-looking and smartly dressed, they were rather conceited and condescending.

She could not help wondering while she was

dancing if perhaps once again the Earl was being tricked by Lady Hester.

"I hope you have enjoyed your first Ball," the Duchess said as they arrived home at two o'clock in the morning.

"Yes, of course, it was wonderful!" Valencia replied. "I know the compliments I was paid I owe entirely to you, Ma'am, because of the gown you gave me, and because of the new way in which my hair has been arranged."

The Duchess laughed.

"You are being far too modest," she said. "It was quite obvious that you were the 'Belle of the Ball.' There was not another young girl there who had your looks or what I can describe only as your *'joie de vivre'!*"

Valencia smiled with delight and the Duchess went on in a different tone of voice:

"At the same time, my dear, you were worried. Is it because of Hue?"

"I was worrying in case Lady Hester was trying to . . . trick him . . . again and perhaps he was not being . . . careful."

The Duchess moved across the room before she said:

"I expect you know that Hue has said he has no intention of being married?"

She paused and smiled at Valencia before continuing:

"In fact, before he went to the country I had a long talk with him, and when I suggested he should take a wife, he told me firmly it was something he had no wish to do."

"I can understand that," Valencia said, "but Lady Hester is determined to marry him so that he can pay off her brother's debts, and I am so afraid that he will be taken off his guard."

"I am quite sure, my dear, that you can leave Hue to look after himself," the Duchess replied. "What is far more important is for us to find you a husband."

Valencia looked startled.

"But I have no wish to be married either," she declared.

"Nonsense!" the Duchess said. "Every girl wants to be married, and it is always wise to marry in your first Season, when you are young and unspoilt, which is what most men require of their wives."

Valencia wanted to ask why, in that case, did they spend so much time with women like Lady Hester?

But she told herself she was very ignorant.

How could she possibly understand a man like the Earl?

She and the Duchess walked up the stairs to-gether, and as they went, the Duchess said again:

"Hue has made up his mind to remain a bachelor and, quite frankly, I think it would be a mistake for you to become so embroiled in his affairs that you spoil your own chances."

"I was thinking only of the Priory," Valencia said, "and how important it is that the Earl should take the place of his cousins who were killed."

"I am sure he will do that admirably," the Duchess said.

She smiled at Valencia before she continued:

"But by the time he has established himself as the head of the family, I want you to have made a life of your own with some charming young man who, I hope, will own a house as fine as the Priory, and whose blood is just as noble."

The Duchess made it sound a very attractive prospect.

Yet Valencia had the idea that nothing could be as lovely or as perfect as the Priory.

What was more, no man she had met so far could rival the Earl in looks.

Or in what she could describe to herself only as "personality."

She had the feeling that he would tower above every other man in any room in which he was present.

That was what drew women like Lady Hester to him, and made them determined to possess him for themselves.

"How can I look after him if I never see him?" she asked in the darkness when she was in bed.

There was no answer to that question.

It was still in her mind when she awoke in the morning.

*   *   *

The whole of the first day after his return to London the Earl had been very busy at the Foreign Office.

He had then enjoyed the Regimental Banquet.

The Prince of Wales had been in great form and made an excellent speech. He had praised the Earl for his valour and the awards he had won which had been a compliment to the whole Regiment.

After it was all over he had then insisted that the Earl drive back with him to Marlborough House.

"Why has living in the country, Dolphinston, been more attractive than the invitations I have been sending you?" he asked truculently.

"I had to explore my new estate, Sir," the Earl replied, "and, in fact, I also discovered there a new Beauty whom I have brought with me to London to be with my grandmother, the Duchess of Wakefield."

"A new Beauty!" the Prince of Wales exclaimed. "Then, of course, I should like to meet her."

"She is very young," the Earl said a little defensively.

"Inevitably she will grow older!" the Prince replied, and they both laughed.

They talked of other things, and when the Earl was leaving Marlborough House, the Prince of Wales said:

"I know the Princess always enjoys the company of your grandmother, so I will send her an invitation to join us after a dinner-party which we are giving on Thursday. She can bring with her your *protégée* from the country."

"Thank you, Sir, that is most gracious of you," the Earl replied.

He drove home thinking that it would certainly be a great experience for Valencia to meet the Prince and Princess of Wales.

It was well known that the Prince was normally interested only in sophisticated and married Beauties.

Therefore, for a young girl to be invited to Marlborough House would make Valencia the envy of her contemporaries.

"I have certainly done my best for her!" the Earl told himself as he went to bed.

Before he went to sleep he thought with satisfaction that since his return to London there had been no sign of Lady Hester.

He hoped that the whole unsavoury episode could be forgotten and he would never see her again.

Nevertheless, he could not help remembering what a dastardly plot it had been to drug and then marry him.

When that had failed, she had threatened him with violence.

"I should never have become involved with the woman in the first place!" the Earl told himself.

It was something he said over and over again.

At the same time, if he were honest, he could not help remembering the fire she had engendered in him.

He tried to tell himself:

"It is all over and I will not think of her."

But he could not dismiss the uncomfortable feeling that it would not be so easy to be rid of Hester.

She would be waiting for her chance, although it seemed fantastic, to pounce on him once again.

* * *

The next morning the Earl told himself he was being ridiculous in wasting his thoughts on anybody so unworthy.

He had learned from his secretary, Mr. Stevenson, that there had been an uncomfortable and rather ugly scene when Lady Hester returned to Park Lane.

She had been told that her luggage was packed and waiting in the hall.

She was informed that in no way could she, her

brother, or Sir Roger be accommodated any longer as the Earl's guests.

The Earl gathered without Mr. Stevenson's saying so in so many words that Edward Ward had been extremely rude to him.

He had also been appalled at the way in which Lady Hester had finally lost her temper.

However, Mr. Stevenson had remained firm.

Their luggage was loaded onto a carriage and driven away from Park Lane, although where they went he had not the slightest idea.

There were a number of people to see the Earl before he could leave the house that morning.

As he had promised to have luncheon with the Foreign Secretary, he had to hurry to Whitehall in case he should be late.

It was only, therefore, at tea-time that he managed to reach his grandmother's house in Belgrave Square and walked into the Drawing-Room unannounced.

The Duchess and Valencia had once again been shopping.

They both looked up with expressions of surprise and Valencia gave a little cry of joy when she saw the Earl.

"You have been neglecting us, Hue!" the Duchess complained. "We have been wondering what had happened to you."

"I have been very busy, Grandmama."

He looked at Valencia. Then he said:

"Who is this beautiful young lady you have with you? I do not believe I have seen her before!"

Valencia laughed.

"That is what we wanted you to say, and please,

tell your grandmother you approve of the transformation, of which I am very conscious."

She jumped up from the sofa on which she had been sitting with the Duchess to show the Earl how she looked in her new gown.

It was a very pretty one of pale blue which matched her eyes, and was trimmed with chiffon ruching round the hem.

It gave her an ethereal look which the Earl thought was very attractive.

It accentuated the smallness of her waist and the slimness of her figure, which had never been so well displayed before.

"You are . . . pleased?"

He knew by the way Valencia spoke that his answer was very important.

He looked towards his grandmother, saying:

"I congratulate you, Grandmama! I always knew your taste was impeccable, and nobody could produce a debutante better than you have once you set your mind to it."

"Thank you!" the Duchess replied. "At the same time, my 'leading lady' has all the attributes which are essential if she is to become a star."

Valencia clasped her hands together.

"If that is what I am, then I do hope you are proud of me."

"Very proud," the Earl affirmed, "and now I would like a cup of tea, as I have had a most exhausting day."

"We have not told you our news," Valencia said.

"And what is that?"

"Your grandmother has been invited to Marlborough House tonight by the Prince and Princess of Wales, and I am included in the invitation!"

"That is what I had hoped for," the Earl said.

"We thought it must be you! Oh, how kind of you! I shall enjoy seeing the Prince and Princess, and it will be something to tell Papa when I go home."

"Are you in such a hurry to leave London?" the Earl enquired.

"No, of course not . . . it is very exciting being here. At the same time, I keep wondering if they are missing me."

"And she also keeps worrying about you!" the Duchess interposed. "I have told the child it is quite unnecessary, but she seems to think you still need a nurse-maid to prevent you from falling out of your perambulator!"

The Earl laughed before he said:

"You need not worry about me, Valencia. There are no gentlemen with revolvers in their hands hiding in the umbrella-stand, and I promise you I am very particular about what I eat and drink."

Valencia drew in her breath before she said:

"You are making a joke of it, but please . . . please . . . be careful! I cannot help feeling that you are not yet out . . . of reach of those people."

"Now, that is being morbid," the Duchess said, "and I am quite certain that Lady Hester, much as I dislike her, is not likely to endanger her social reputation by making people aware not only of how she has behaved, but how she has failed."

"You are quite right," the Earl agreed, "and there-fore, as I have said before, I want Valencia to enjoy herself and think only of herself and forget about me.

It is something in which she should never have been involved in the first place!"

"Of course she should not," the Duchess agreed, "and I hope you are listening, Valencia."

"Yes, Ma'am, I am listening!" Valencia said.

But as she looked at the Earl she fancied that just behind him like a shadow was Lady Hester.

She was watching and waiting, like a tigress, determined sooner or later to spring on her prey.

It was then, as a steel of fear flashed through her heart, that she knew she loved him.

chapter six

"How can I be so ridiculous?" Valencia asked herself as she found it impossible to sleep.

It seemed unrealistic that she should have fallen in love with the Earl, when she had at first disapproved of the way he was behaving.

She had also been shocked at his association with Lady Hester.

She could understand, in a way, although she was very innocent, that men needed the company of a woman.

If she was as beautiful as Lady Hester, it was inevitable they would wish to kiss and make love to her.

What that entailed Valencia was not certain.

But she knew that the love she had seen between her father and her mother was what she wanted for herself.

She prayed she would be fortunate enough to find it.

Yet, incredibly, she had fallen in love with a man who just found her useful in getting to know his property.

She sensed in his avowed determination not to marry that he was equally determined to have as little as possible to do with respectable young women like herself.

She was not certain how she knew this.

Yet just as she could read the Earl's thoughts, so at other times she was aware of his feelings.

It seemed very strange, but when he spoke about Lady Hester, she thought he revealed that he resented her behaviour.

As a woman he also regarded her with contempt.

She was so beautiful, but Valencia was sure that was what he felt.

Because she, too, was a woman, she thought perhaps he felt the same way about her.

She was very intelligent and she realised, when she thought things over, that it was only to be expected that she would fall in love with the Earl.

Living quietly in the country with her father, she had seen so few men, and he was irresistible.

However, since she had come to London she had met a large number of them.

She knew that not one compared in any way with the Earl either in looks, intelligence, or personality.

"I suppose he is unique," she told herself miserably, "and what I am feeling is just hero-worship."

Then she knew it was much more than that.

Now she understood why the parties when the Earl was not present seemed rather dull.

Why, when he was there, it was impossible to listen to anyone who was talking to her.

"I love him!"

The words seemed to echo round her bed-room.

She knew that his loving her was as likely as that she would be flown to the moon.

'Whatever happens,' she thought, 'he will soon be no longer interested in me, and I expect all I shall see of him is when he is riding in the Park, as I saw him the first time.'

She could remember how impressive he had seemed.

How she had been quite certain, even though there was nobody to tell her so, that he was the Earl, and not the man accompanying him.

She had felt, too, when he was unconscious, that he had looked younger and more vulnerable.

Although she had not realised it was love, she had wanted to look after him and protect him.

She wanted to prevent Lady Hester, or anybody else, from hurting him.

She finally went to sleep, and when she woke up, it was to see his face in front of her eyes.

She found herself sending her thoughts towards him as if they were carried on the wings of a dove.

"You are looking rather pale, my dear," the Duchess said when they met later in the morning. "I think you should rest this afternoon, as I want you to look your very best at Marlborough House this evening."

"It will be very exciting to see the Prince and Princess of Wales," Valencia answered.

But she knew that what she was really looking forward to was seeing the Earl.

He was more important to her than all the Princes in the world.

There was a small, but select, luncheon-party to enjoy first.

Although there were several distinguished young aristocrats present, it was difficult for Valencia to concentrate on what they were saying to her.

"I am sure you liked Lord Fenwick," the Duchess said.

They were driving back to Belgrave Square in her carriage.

Valencia must have looked blank because she went on:

"He was sitting on your right at luncheon, and I thought he was being very attentive."

"Oh, yes, of course," Valencia agreed. "I remember him now."

The Duchess laughed.

"Lord Fenwick is sought after by all the debutantes. He is very wealthy and his mother tells me he is looking for a suitable wife."

"I wonder what he means by 'suitable,'" Valencia said.

"As he has had some rather lurid *affaires de coeur* with married women," the Duchess replied, "I am sure he is looking for an attractive young woman who is not spoilt and will be a gracious hostess in his many different houses."

She paused before continuing:

"She must also, of course, provide him with an heir, in fact, several, just to be on the safe side!"

Valencia gave a little shudder.

"It sounds so matter-of-fact and businesslike when put like that," she said. "If I marry, I would wish to marry a man who . . . loves me just . . . because I am . . . me!"

The Duchess smiled.

"That is what we all want, but it is an idealistic love which we read about in books, hear in music, and, of course, in poetry, but which rarely happens in real life."

She stopped and looked at Valencia before she went on:

"That is why, dear child, you should take the best that is offered and not be too fastidious."

"But I could never marry . . . anyone unless I . . . loved them!" Valencia cried.

Even as she spoke she knew that condemned her to remain an Old Maid.

While she loved the Earl, he would never love her.

Therefore she would devote the rest of her life to caring for her father.

She must forget the Social World in which she and the Earl were as far apart as the North and the South Poles.

"I have invited Lord Fenwick to dine with us next Wednesday," the Duchess said, who was following her own chain of thought. "I do so beg of you, dearest child, to be charming to him. I should be very proud, very proud indeed, if you were to marry the 'catch of the Season'!"

Valencia shut her eyes for a moment and told herself it would be a mistake to answer.

How could she ever explain to the Duchess, who was so kind to her, that she did not want the "catch of the Season"?

But she wanted only one man—and he was as far out of reach as if he lived on the moon.

When they arrived back at Belgrave Square the Duchess insisted that Valencia go upstairs and lie down.

"I have learnt that several of my friends have also been invited to Marlborough House after dinner, and there will be music and perhaps dancing."

She paused before she finished:

"I have, therefore, asked them to dine here first, but I am afraid, my dear, they are all very much older than you."

"Please do not worry about me," Valencia said. "You are so kind and I realise it is a great privilege to be going to Marlborough House. Of course I am . . . very grateful."

*   *   *

When Valencia began to dress after she had had her bath and was deciding which of her new gowns she should wear, she was wondering if the Earl would admire her.

It did not concern her what anybody else thought.

The Duchess finally decided she should wear a gown that was very unusual.

It was certainly a frame for her particular looks.

Of white lace with a touch of silver, it was decorated round the hem and over the shoulders with white flowers, which were particularly suitable for a debutante.

To add a touch of sophistication, each flower had a glittering diamond on its petals and its leaves, as if they were drops of rain.

What again made it different were the long very pale green gloves that went with it, and also little satin slippers in the same colour.

"You look lovely, dear child," the Duchess said when Valencia joined her in the Drawing-Room before dinner, "and I know His Royal Highness will think so too."

Valencia smiled.

"I doubt he will even notice me. Your lady's-maid was telling me while she was arranging my hair that the Prince is infatuated with the beautiful Lady Brook."

Valencia laughed.

"Her gowns glitter all over with diamanté and she is so lovely that crowds gather outside her house just to see her."

"That is true," the Duchess admitted, "and Daisy is so sweet that everybody loves her."

There was a little pause, then Valencia said:

"What I do not . . . understand is why Lord Brooke is not jealous of the Prince of Wales paying so much attention . . . to his . . . wife."

The Duchess did not answer for a moment, then she said:

"Lord Brooke is very fond of His Royal Highness and enjoys entertaining him at shooting-parties and on many other social occasions."

She realised Valencia still did not understand.

She quickly talked of something else, and Lady Brooke was forgotten.

But the dinner-party was not so discreet.

Because Valencia was so much younger than everybody else, the gentlemen on either side of her, after paying her a few compliments, talked to the ladies on the other side of them.

She heard one say:

"I suppose Daisy will be there tonight looking even more glamorous than usual, but I find it quite embarrassing to see the expression in the Prince's eyes when he looks at her."

"Princess Alexandra is so sensible about it," the lady to whom he was speaking replied. "If he were my husband, I should want to throw something at him! But the Princess just smiles, though I cannot help feeling it must be rather galling."

There was silence for a moment, then the lady went on:

"But you men are all the same, except that most of you are more discreet and remember the Eleventh Commandment—'Thou shalt not be found out!'"

There was laughter at this.

Valencia, listening, suddenly felt that perhaps the reason why they had seen so little of the Earl was that he, like the Prince of Wales, had found somebody new to love.

Someone with whom he could have what the Duchess referred to as an *affaire de coeur* without it involving him in marriage.

The whole idea was like a sharp knife in her breast.

Quite suddenly she wanted to go home.

She had felt an outsider in the Social World, and now she knew it not only frightened but hurt her.

'These people do not understand and perhaps will never know the happiness Papa and Mama had together,' she thought, 'and as that is the sort of happiness I want, it is no use my staying here amongst them and torturing myself.'

She remembered how the Earl had said that if she wanted to return home after a few weeks in London he would not prevent her from doing so.

"I will go back to Papa," she decided, "and provided I can ride, I shall be happy without dinner-parties and Balls, and meeting a lot of rather stupid young men who mean nothing to me."

"You are looking very pensive, Miss Hadley," one of the men sitting beside her said unexpectedly. "What are you thinking about?"

"I was thinking of the country," Valencia replied truthfully, "and feeling rather home-sick."

He looked at her in surprise. Then he said:

"That is something I often feel myself. I would much rather be in the country than in London, where I have to attend parties night after night."

"Then why do you do it?" Valencia asked.

"The answer to that is quite simple," he replied. "I have a wife who insists that I 'do the Season,' as it is called. But I shall be in Buckinghamshire in July before we go to Scotland in August."

It struck Valencia that in this social life the same people kept moving all together to different places each month of the year.

It was the only way they could avoid being bored.

Perhaps they deliberately exhausted themselves so as not to think too much.

'That is what I am doing,' she thought. 'Thinking

about the Earl when I should be enjoying myself, and as this is something I shall never do again, I ought to savour every minute of it.'

Then she knew that her thoughts had just gone round in a circle.

She came back to the starting point, which was that she loved the Earl and nothing else was of any importance.

They lingered over dinner.

Because Valencia was longing to see the Earl, it seemed as if a century of time passed before it was over.

Finally they stepped into one of the carriages which was waiting outside and drove off to Marlborough House.

She felt her heart beating faster and a shaft of excitement pierced through her.

It was not because she was going to this most sought-after house.

But it was because among the other guests would be the only person who mattered.

"I will see him, he will talk to me, and perhaps admire me . . . just a little," she told herself.

*   *   *

The dinner at Marlborough House had, as usual, been excellent.

Also, as the Earl had reluctantly anticipated, Lady Hester was among the guests.

She was certainly looking extremely beautiful.

It was not surprising that every man with the exception of himself had paid her compliments before dinner.

Now the two men on either side of her were vying with each other to hold her attention.

She was wearing an obviously very expensive gown of ruby-red tulle which the Earl suspected he had paid for.

It sparkled and glittered with every move she made.

She had a tiara of rubies and diamonds in her hair and a necklace of the same stones, which made her magnolia skin even more sensational than usual.

She was beautiful—the Earl was well aware of that!

At the same time, no one knew as he did what lay beneath the surface.

He knew that any feeling he had for her had now turned to disgust at her wicked lack of scruples.

He had the feeling, because he was very perceptive, that while he had hoped she was no longer interested in him, he had been over-optimistic.

Their eyes met once or twice.

There was an expression in hers which told him all too clearly that she was still thinking of him.

She was still wondering how she could get him back into her clutches.

"That is something which will never happen again!" the Earl assured himself.

To avoid thinking of Lady Hester, he applied himself to appreciating the witty if slightly caustic remarks of the lady on his right.

Then he tried to attract the attention of Lady Brooke, who was on his left.

He realised that because she was on the right of

the Prince of Wales, he himself was in a place of honour.

The Prince had, in fact, shown him a friendship which was the envy of every man present.

When he arrived at Marlborough House, the Prince had held out his hand, saying:

"It is good to see you, Dolphinston, I enjoyed our evening with the Regiment more than I have enjoyed anything for a long time."

"That is very kind of you, Sir," the Earl said. "I also enjoyed myself."

"It is something we must do again," the Prince said, "and the Princess will ask you tonight to come to stay with us at Sandringham."

"I would be very honoured, Sir!" the Earl replied.

He moved away as the Prince was greeted by some other guests who had just arrived.

Lady Brooke must have learned from the Prince about the Earl's distinguished career in the Army in India.

She talked to him of her own interest in the Orient.

Then she said:

"I hope you will come to stay with us at Easton, the week-end after next, when His Royal Highness will be there."

She paused before she continued:

"He is so delighted at everything you have told him about your time in India, and wants to learn more, especially about 'The Great Game.'"

"That is supposed to be a secret!" the Earl remarked.

"I am very discreet, and I hope you will not have too many secrets from me!" Lady Brooke replied.

She looked very lovely as she spoke and had such a charming and sweet way about her.

The Earl thought it was very unlikely that any man could keep secret anything she wanted to know.

It was not surprising, he thought, that the Prince had lost his heart.

It was obviously difficult for him to take his eyes from anyone so exquisite.

At the same time, Daisy Brooke had such a kind nature that she was loved by women as well as men.

At the far end of the table Princess Alexandra was looking exceedingly beautiful, as she always did.

She wore a gown of silver-grey, and a profusion of pearls, which made her regal as well as lovely.

It would be difficult to describe to an outsider, the Earl thought, the charm of Marlborough House.

The Princed had gathered together a diverse collection of people who all had the same thing in common—they were intelligent, witty, and amusing.

When the ladies had left the room, the conversation became political.

The Earl realised, as he had before, how much the Prince resented being kept out of State Affairs by Queen Victoria.

He wanted, in his own words, to be "in the know."

He loathed the fact that he had no official status and was not allowed to see State Papers.

Furthermore, he was told nothing of what was discussed at Cabinet meetings on what the Queen thought was her own prerogative.

The Earl, therefore, like others of his friends, tried to think of subjects in which the Prince could participate.

How he could learn something of what he was not already aware.

From politics they turned to horses, and from horses to women.

Then His Royal Highness decided it was time to join the ladies.

They were waiting for them in the large Drawing-Room.

A little later they would be entertained by an Opera Singer and a String Orchestra that had just captured the imagination and applause of London.

The Prince went ahead, but the Earl was stopped by the Foreign Secretary, Lord Derby, who said to him:

"I must see you tomorrow, Dolphinston. Something has come up with regard to the trouble on the border of Afghanistan which I think you might be able to explain to me."

"What has happened?" the Earl asked sharply.

The Foreign Secretary told him in a low voice that there had been more Russian infiltration.

Secret despatches suggested an uprising amongst the tribesmen.

"I want you to see the papers and tell me what you think will happen," Lord Derby said.

"Of course, if I can be of any help to you," the Earl replied, "I will be only too delighted."

"You have been a great help to me already," Lord Derby said, "and quite frankly, Dolphinston, I am exceedingly grateful."

The Earl and Lord Derby then realised that all the other gentlemen had gone into the Drawing Room.

Feeling it was slightly rude to linger behind, they moved forward.

Each of the gentlemen had already joined the lady of his choice.

As the Earl entered the Drawing-Room he saw at the far end Lady Hester talking intensely to the Prince of Wales.

There was something in her attitude and the way the Prince was listening to her which made the Earl apprehensive.

Then, as he moved forward, he saw her glance towards him and instantly a perceptive part of his brain registered danger.

He knew Lady Hester well enough to be aware exactly what she was feeling at this moment.

He knew it was one of triumph and at the same time of anticipated vengeance.

As this all flashed through his mind, the Prince turned his head and beckoned him.

The feeling of danger persisted as he walked towards the Prince, but he had no choice but to obey the Royal signal.

As he reached the Prince his eyes met Lady Hester's.

He knew by the expression on her face she was confident that once again he was in her power.

Like a leopardess, with which he had identified her before, she would spring and capture him as her prey.

He would not be able to escape.

Then as the Prince began to speak, the Earl knew what she had done.

"My dear Dolphinston," the Prince said genially, "I am delighted, absolutely delighted, because Lady Hester has just been telling me . . ."

As the Prince spoke in his rather thick voice the Earl realised only too clearly how Hester, with her usual disregard of moral scruple, was poised for victory.

He felt the trumpet of doom had sounded and he was completely and utterly annihilated.

Suddenly he saw his grandmother, the Duchess, being greeted by the Princess and behind her came Valencia.

With the swiftness of a man who had faced danger a dozen times before and survived, he interrupted the Prince with an imperative:

"Forgive me, Sir, but I have something of the utmost importance to tell you."

Without waiting for the Prince's reply, he hurried across the room.

As Valencia, having curtsied to the Princess, moved away to follow the Duchess, he reached her side.

Taking her by the hand, he said sharply:

"Come with me!"

She looked at him in surprise.

At the same time, she was conscious of a little quiver running through her simply because he was touching her.

As he drew her across the room to where the Prince was waiting, he said to her in a low voice so that only she could hear:

"Save me, Valencia, save me, for God's sake!"

She looked at him in astonishment, then they were beside the Prince.

The Earl deliberately came to a standstill.

He was in a position where His Royal Highness was obliged almost to turn his back on Lady Hester.

"May I present, Sir," the Earl said, "the new Beauty whom Your Royal Highness was kind enough to invite here this evening in the company of my grandmother."

The Prince put out his hand, and as Valencia took it and curtsied to the ground, he said:

"You were right, Dolphinston, as you always are! She is beautiful! Absolutely beautiful!"

The Earl drew a little closer and said very quietly:

"It is a secret, Sir, which must for the moment be known only to you, but Valencia Hadley is in fact my wife!"

There was a moment's silence.

The Prince looked at the Earl in astonishment and Valencia drew in her breath.

Then she understood and knew that to save the Earl, as he had implored her to do, she must co-operate.

She was, however, startled and a little shocked that he should lie in such a strange manner.

"This is indeed a surprise!" the Prince was saying.

"I will explain it to you later, Sir, when we cannot be overheard, why it is important that absolutely no-one should know of this except, of course, yourself."

The Prince was delighted.

That he should be the first to know of any secret always intrigued him.

He was very conscious that there must be some interesting, if for the moment inexplicable, reason that the Earl should be secretive about his marriage.

For the moment Lady Hester had been forgotten.

Then, as the Earl met her eyes glaring at him like those of a wild animal, he knew she had heard—as, of course, he had intended—what he had said.

From her point of view he had turned victory into defeat.

Two new-comers came up to speak to the Prince, and while he was greeting them the Earl drew Valencia away.

As he did so, Valencia looked up at him enquiringly, and he said:

"Later, when we are away from here, I will explain."

As it happened, he had no chance to say any more.

The Duchess came up to speak to her grandson and there were several young people to whom she wished to introduce Valencia.

One of whom was specially fulsome in his compliments.

More and more people were arriving, several of whom knew the Earl and quite a number the Duchess.

Since for Valencia there was no question of being able to talk to him, she was trying to figure out what had happened.

She, in fact, came very near the truth.

It was only when they had listened to an excellent Opera Singer that the Band struck up a lively Waltz.

The Earl quickly asked Valencia to dance.

Then, as they moved over the polished floor, he said quietly:

"Thank you for saving me for the third time, Valencia!"

"What . . . happened? I was . . . afraid when I saw . . . Lady Hester."

"Not half as frightened as I was!" he replied. "I will tell you all about it later, but not here."

The dance was a very short one.

After leaving her with the Duchess, the Earl danced with the Princess.

Then with several other beautiful women without asking her again.

She had plenty of partners.

At the same time, her whole body was throbbing because the Earl had said she was his wife.

She knew it was untrue and obviously invented merely as a way of circumventing some plot that Lady Hester had been hatching as they entered the room.

Just to look at her dancing with a feline grace made Valencia aware how dangerous she was.

Also how frightening the future, when the Earl must always be on his guard.

'I must learn exactly what happened,' she thought.

It was not possible while she was at Marlborough House.

*   *   *

It was long after midnight when they drove back in the Duchess's carriage.

Valencia was aware that the Earl did not wish to speak in front of his grandmother.

He had asked if he could join them.

He had arranged for his own carriage to follow them to Belgrave Square.

The Duchess had seemed slightly surprised, but she had, of course, agreed.

When the carriage started off from Marlborough House she asked:

"Are you making up for having neglected us all day, Hue? I thought you were having luncheon with us."

"I wanted to," the Earl replied, "but as you probably guessed, I was at the War Office, then the Foreign Office."

He paused before he went on:

"If you want the truth, I am tired of answering questions which the 'powers that be' should know without my having to tell them!"

The Duchess laughed.

"Such is fame! And you know you would be furious if they did not consult you!"

"That is true," the Earl admitted, "but I have had nearly enough of it, and the sooner I can go back to the country, the better!"

Valencia felt her heart turn over at the idea that he wanted to go back to the Priory.

Then she told herself it was not to see her but, she was sure, merely to escape from Lady Hester.

It did not take long for them to reach Belgrave Square.

As the Duchess got out she asked:

"Are you coming in for a drink, Hue?"

"If you will offer me one."

"You know the answer to that," she replied.

They walked into the hall and as the night-footman took the Earl's cloak, the Duchess said:

"Bring us some champagne to the Blue Room."

"Very good, M'Lady."

The Blue Room was an Ante-room off one of the Drawing-Rooms which the Duchess and Valencia used when there were no guests.

It was a small, lovely room with some very fine pictures, and a log fire was burning in the grate.

The Duchess looked round almost as if she were seeing that everything was in order.

Then she said:

"I have a feeling, Hue, that you really want to talk to Valencia. So, unless you particularly want me to stay, I am going to bed because I am tired."

"I think that is very wise," the Earl said, "and I will not stay long, I promise you."

The Duchess kissed Valencia, saying:

"Good-night, dear child. I hope you enjoyed your first evening with the most attractive Royal couple in Europe."

"Of course I did," Valencia replied, "and thank you very much for taking me there. It was very exciting, and something I shall always remember."

The Duchess looked pleased.

Then she kissed her grandson, saying:

"Do not keep Valencia up too late. She has another party tomorrow night, where once again I intend she shall be the 'Belle of the Ball.'"

"There will be no doubt about that!" the Earl said.

He escorted his grandmother to the foot of the stairs, then came back into the Blue Room.

Valencia was standing in front of the fire where he had left her.

As he shut the door she clasped her fingers together and asked in a frightened little voice:

"What . . . happened? I felt . . . in fact . . . I was sure that you were in . . . danger."

"You were right," the Earl said.

He walked towards her and as he did so the door opened and the footman came in with the bottle of champagne in an ice-cooler.

He set it down on a table, and the Earl said:

"Leave it. I will pour it."

"Very good, M'Lord."

The footman withdrew, and the Earl, having poured out two glasses of champagne, carried one to Valencia.

She hesitated before she took it from him, and he said:

"Take it, I think you are going to need it."

He saw her eyes widen in fear as she took the glass and sat down on the sofa.

"What h-happened?" she asked again.

"When I went into the Drawing-Room after dinner, I saw Lady Hester talking to His Royal Highness and instinctively I knew she was telling him that she and I were engaged to be married."

"Engaged?" Valencia exclaimed. "How could she do that? How could he believe it?"

"Very easily," the Earl replied. "Before I came down to the Priory, I had been stupid enough not to realise that when the most acknowledged Beauty in the Social World had been staying with me at my house in London and entertaining at the end of my table, everyone would expect our marriage to be announced."

He paused before he said:

"I wonder now how I could have been such a fool as not to be aware of what I was doing! My only excuse is that I was extremely busy, and I thought at the time that Lady Hester was very necessary to me."

"I . . . understand," Valencia said in a low voice.

"Never did I suppose that she would expect me to marry her," the Earl went on, "and I had no intention of marrying anyone who—"

He stopped, feeling that what he had been about to say would be indiscreet.

It was certainly unfit for the ears of anyone as young as Valencia.

He drank a little of his champagne and put the glass down before he went on:

"It was only when I came to the Priory that Lady Hester made it clear what she expected, and you know what happened then."

His voice was sharp as he continued:

"I thought when I drove Lady Hester, her brother, and Sir Roger Crawford out of the Priory and from my house in London, that I had seen the last of them."

"I had a feeling she . . . would not . . . give up so easily . . . ," Valencia murmured.

"You were right," the Earl answered, "and tonight she played her 'trump card' which, had it not been for your presence, would have won her the trick!"

"I . . . I do not . . . understand . . ."

"I saw her talking to His Royal Highness, and as I reached them, he started to congratulate me on my engagement to Lady Hester!"

"I was . . . afraid that was . . . what had . . . happened," Valencia said.

"It was doubly clever," the Earl said, "because she is aware, as indeed we all are, that the Prince not only cannot resist being 'first in the know,' but also, because as he himself is in love, he is only too willing to assist in any romantic episode amongst his friends."

Valencia, listening, raised her eyes to the Earl's face.

He could see that she was still worried.

"It was when His Royal Highness was about to congratulate me that I saw you in the doorway and knew you were my salvation."

"It was clever of you," Valencia said, "but do you think he . . . believed . . . you?"

"He believed me," the Earl said grimly, "but Lady Hester will do her utmost to prove it is a lie."

"Then . . . what can . . . you do?" Valencia asked.

"I should have thought that was obvious," the Earl replied. "We must get married—and quickly!"

chapter seven

Driving through the traffic in the Earl's Phaeton drawn by four perfectly matched horses, Valencia felt she must be dreaming.

It was as if she had not been able to breathe ever since the moment the Earl had said incredibly:

"We must get married—and quickly!"

She had stared at him then as if she thought she could not have heard right.

Almost as if he were accusing her of stupidity, he said:

"It is obvious! We can do nothing else! Hester has already informed the Prince that we are engaged."

He smiled at her before he continued:

"Although he must have been surprised—one might almost say bewildered—by learning that we are married, I shall have to substantiate it, not only to him, but also to Lady Hester and her disreputable brother!"

Valencia had moved her lips, intending to say she could not marry him, but no words would come.

He took her hand and said as if he were thinking it out in his agile brain:

"We leave for the country very early in the morning. Your father will marry us."

He paused to look at her then went on:

"I am sure somehow you can contrive that the date in the Register can be made earlier for any 'busy-bodies' who will undoubtedly come looking at it."

Valencia understood what he was saying.

At the same time, she felt as if her head was full of cotton-wool.

It was impossible either to argue or to agree in words.

She could only stand listening, as if she had been turned to stone.

"What you have to do now," the Earl said as if he were giving orders before a battle, "is to go upstairs and tell the maid who helps you dress that you will be leaving tomorrow morning at seven o'clock."

He stopped, then explained:

"She is to pack your clothes, which will be collected by my Valet and placed in another vehicle from the one in which we shall travel."

Only as the Earl finished speaking did Valencia ask in a voice that did not sound like her own:

"What . . . what about your . . . grandmother?"

"You can leave her a note saying that you were obliged to go home with me for a while, and that I will explain everything to her later. In the meantime, you deeply regret having to cancel your engagements for tomorrow and the next day."

"But . . . what reason shall . . . I give?"

"Say it was imperative that you obey my request."

Afterwards Valencia was to think there was no chance of her doing anything else, when the Earl said:

"I am grateful, exceedingly grateful to you, Valencia. I know that you understand it would be impossible after what has occured for me to contemplate marrying Lady Hester, which I shall be obliged to do if you do not save me."

There were a dozen questions Valencia wanted to ask him.

He had, however, merely raised her hand to his lips, kissed it, and said:

"Go to bed now. It may seem frightening to you, but everything will sort itself out with, of course, your help."

He smiled at her in a manner that was irresistible.

Before she could say anything, before she could beg him not to leave her, he had gone from the room.

He shut the door behind him, leaving her alone.

Only when she walked slowly up the stairs to find the maid waiting for her did she remember his instructions.

Almost as if she were a puppet being pulled by strings she did what he had ordered her to do.

But as she got into bed she was shivering.

Not from the cold but because she was afraid of everything that had happened.

Most of all, she was afraid of marrying the Earl.

"How can I . . . marry him," she asked herself,

"when he does not love me... and I am only... a way out of a... trap?"

At the same time, somewhere inside her heart there was an irresistible excitement.

If she were married to the Earl, she would at least be able to be with him.

She could see him, talk to him, and listen to him as she wanted to do.

Although he might never reciprocate her love or even be aware of it, she would not lose him completely.

She knew, however, that it would be an agony to be with him when he not only had no love for her, but she was not the type of woman who attracted him.

She had only to think of Lady Hester, of her beautiful face, her sensuous body, her sharp but amusing and witty tongue, to know that she appealed to the Earl physically.

Valencia felt she would never even hold his interest.

"I love him! I love him!" she whispered in the darkness.

They were words of despair.

Strangely enough, although she had expected to lie awake for hours thinking, she slept from sheer emotional exhaustion.

* * *

Valencia was awoken by the maid calling her as she had been told to do at six o'clock.

After a late night the Duchess ordered her breakfast at nine-thirty.

Valencia thought the Earl must have been aware of this and that was why he intended to collect her long before his grandmother was awake.

She wrote the note as he had instructed her, then dressed herself carefully in one of her beautiful new gowns.

There was a coat trimmed with white braid to wear over it.

She thought it completed one of the most elegant *ensembles* she had ever imagined.

With it there was a high-crowned bonnet trimmed with blue ribbon which matched her eyes.

It made her look very young and at the same time extremely lovely.

It gave her the confidence to walk to where the Earl was waiting for her without being as frightened as she might otherwise have been.

He was waiting in the hall.

He looked very smart with his cravat tied in a new and intricate style.

His coat fitted without a wrinkle, and as they walked outside he set his tall hat at a raffish angle on his dark hair.

Valencia had already had a chance to admire his Phaeton when he had come to luncheon.

She was aware that it was more up-to-date than any other she had seen when driving with the Duchess in Rotten Row.

The four chestnuts were a new acquisition and were so well-bred that Valencia longed to have time to inspect them.

The Earl, however, helped her quickly into the Phaeton before he settled himself in the driving-seat.

She knew he was in a hurry.

The groom sprang up behind and they drove in silence until they were out of London.

Then the Earl said:

"I sent a groom at dawn to your father, informing him of our arrival."

He paused before he continued:

"I have said that I wished to see him urgently on a matter pertaining to the Church Register, which is not to be shown to anybody before our arrival."

Valencia looked at him in astonishment.

"Why, do you think . . . anybody will . . . want to do . . . that?"

"For a very intelligent young woman you are being rather obtuse. Of course Lady Hester or her abominable brother will make an effort to see if what I said last night to the Prince of Wales is true."

"Of course they would! I had not . . . thought of that . . . !" Valencia said humbly.

They drove on and she wondered what her father would think when he learnt that they were to be married so suddenly.

Also, she questioned as to whether the Earl would tell him the truth.

She tried to think out reasonable answers.

But after a while she was just content to sit beside the Earl, giving him occasionally a sideways glance.

It was impossible for a man to look more handsome and distinguished, or, in fact, more exciting.

'If only he . . . loved me,' she thought.

Then she knew that she was being greedy.

She had prayed that she would not have to leave the Earl too soon and that he would not forget her.

Now both wishes had been granted.

To ask that he should love her, too, was demanding the impossible.

Yet that was what she wanted.

"Please . . . God, please," she prayed, "just let him . . . love me . . . a little."

It did not strike her until they were actually driving into the Priory grounds that in marrying the Earl she would be the mistress of a house which had always meant so much to her.

Now she would be able to preserve the old customs.

She could keep the servants happy who had been there for so many years.

She might, if she was tactful, persuade the Earl to carry out many improvements.

Some were very necessary in the village and in other parts of the estate.

For a moment she felt quite giddy that such things were in her hands.

Then she knew because the Earl did not love her that she must consider him and not her own feelings in the matter.

Just before they reached the front-door, the Earl, who had been concentrating on his driving, said:

"I know you will want to change and I thought it would be easier if you did so at the Priory rather than in your house. I want us to be married, if possible, within the hour."

Valencia looked at him incredulously, but before she could argue or ask questions, he had drawn the horses to a standstill.

As the servants came hurrying towards them he said:

"Have Miss Hadley's luggage taken up to the Queen's Room the moment it arrives."

The Butler to whom he had given the order was too well trained to look surprised.

But Valencia, as she went up the stairs, knew that the whole household would be wondering what was happening.

Why, they would ask her, had she not gone home to her father.

It was typical, she thought, that with the Earl's organisation everything had been arranged in advance.

Breakfast was brought to her in the Queen's Room before she had even taken off her bonnet.

There were a Housekeeper and two maids to wait on her.

They opened her trunk when it arrived only five minutes later, and asked which of her gowns she would wear.

Valencia hesitated.

Then she chose the one in which the Duchess had intended to present her at Buckingham Palace.

It was, of course, white and very beautifully trimmed with chiffon frilling and real lace.

It also had a train which Valencia felt was appropriate.

At the same time, her head was in a whirl.

She did not know what to say or even what to think.

She was aware only that she must obey the Earl's instructions to the letter.

She bathed in water scented with oil of violets which had been distilled at the Priory for generations.

She put on her gown and one of the maids arranged her hair in the style she had worn it in London.

Then she looked into the mirror wondering what she could wear on her head.

There was a knock on the door, and when the Housekeeper opened it a footman handed her something.

Valencia saw a tiara shaped like a crown so that it encircled the whole of the head of the wearer.

Beneath it on the tray on which it rested lay a veil.

Valencia stared at it.

She was thinking it very indiscreet of the Earl to let the servants know they were about to be married.

But before she could speak the Housekeeper said:

"His Lordship says to tell you, Miss, that the photographer will be waiting for you downstairs in the Charles II Room where he says the light's better."

There was a faint smile on Valencia's lips as she understood what the Earl was planning.

He was trying to ensure that she felt like a bride, because she was one, but no one must realise it.

It was to appear that she was being photographed and the Charles II Room was next to the Chapel.

"His Lordship remarked last time he was here that you, Miss, are very like the portrait of the Countess Anne which hangs in the Gallery, and that's true," the Housekeeper remarked.

She paused before she continued:

"At the same time, I remember your dear mother,

God rest her soul, had an even greater resemblance to the lady who did so much for the Priory."

It was the Countess Anne, Valencia knew, who had made the Priory so beautiful, as it still was today.

She had embroidered with her own hands the altar-cloth beneath which she and Ben had hidden so that they could save the Earl.

"I am very proud to resemble the Countess Anne," she replied. "She must have been a remarkable person!"

"And a very beautiful one, Miss, as you'll look wearing the tiara and her wedding-veil."

The wedding-veil was not placed over Valencia's face, but floated down over her shoulders.

As she looked at herself in the mirror she hoped that perhaps because she resembled the Countess Anne the Earl would admire her.

She was praying for him to do so, when there was another knock on the door.

"His Lordship's waiting, Miss!" the footman announced.

"There's no need to ask you, Miss Valencia, if you knows the way," the Housekeeper said, smiling, "and we've been told to keep out of sight while you're being photographed, as the gentleman's temperamental and doesn't like to be disturbed."

"I suppose all photographers are like that," Valencia said.

She felt she must play up to this charade which the Earl had invented.

She was not quite certain why he had done so.

It would have been much easier if they had just

got married in the clothes in which they had come down from London.

But she supposed he had his reasons.

She went down the staircase which Lady Hester had discovered led to the Chapel.

The Charles II Room was on one side of it.

Valencia was not surprised when she reached the foot of the stairs to find that the Earl was waiting for her.

He had changed and looked very smart and handsome.

As she reached the last step he put out his hand to take hers and said:

"You look exactly as I wanted you to."

Because she could not help teasing him, she said:

"To be . . . photographed?"

"To be married!" he corrected quietly.

He put her arm through his. As they moved towards the Chapel, Valencia asked:

"Are you . . . quite certain you . . . must do this? Would it not be . . . better if we just went on . . . pretending and . . . lying?"

Her voice trembled on the last word, and the Earl replied:

"No, Valencia, we are to be married, and your father is waiting for us."

There was nothing more she could say.

As they walked into the Chapel she saw her father standing in front of the altar.

Then she was sure that her mother was near her, telling her that everything would be all right.

Yet she was being married in very strange circumstances.

As she moved up the aisle, her train rustling behind her, she thought this must be only a dream.

In a moment she would wake up and the Earl would have vanished.

She would find herself at home in her own bed having dreamt everything that had occurred from the moment she had overheard Lady Hester and her brother plotting in the Chapel.

Then as she and the Earl reached the altar-steps, her father smiled at her.

She thought he was glad that he was to marry her.

He began the Marriage Service, reading the beautiful prayers in his grave, sincere voice.

Valencia was sure that not only was her mother near her, but that she could hear the music of angel voices.

There was a light in the Chapel that shone through the stained-glass windows.

The Earl put the wedding-ring on her finger.

As he said, "With my body I thee worship," Valencia trembled.

Then her father blessed them.

As he did so she sent out another fervent prayer that the Earl would love her just a little.

She felt that her love for him was pouring towards him like the rays of the sun.

"I love . . . him! I . . . love him!" she whispered in her heart. "Please God . . . make him . . . love me."

The Earl raised Valencia's hand to his lips.

"You have saved me for the third, and last time," he said very quietly, "and later I will tell you how grateful I am."

To Valencia's surprise they went back to her home.

They walked down the underground passage, her father guiding them with a lantern which he collected from the Vestry.

They entered the house to find Nanny waiting to put her arms around Valencia and kiss her.

The old woman was very near to tears, and Valencia said:

"You should have been in the Chapel, Nanny."

"I had plenty to do here," Nanny replied, "and you look lovely, Miss Valencia, just as your mother would have wanted, and she'd be real proud to know you're now the mistress of the Priory."

They went into the Study, where there was champagne.

The Earl insisted that Nanny also have a glass before she hurried away to her kitchen.

Her father toasted their health and the Earl replied, saying:

"This is a very happy day for us all, Vicar, and I know that Valencia will be not only the loveliest of all the Countesses who have reigned at the Priory, but also the most efficient."

He paused to laugh before continuing:

"In fact, I am quite frightened of all the things she will insist upon my doing and be very critical of anything I leave undone!"

Her father laughed, but Valencia blushed.

She thought perhaps the Earl was suggesting that she would be too much of a "busybody."

A few minutes later Nanny said that luncheon was ready.

Without changing, Valencia went into the Dining-Room.

She felt surprised that it was much later than she thought, as everything had been done in such a rush.

Only when the meal, which was a light one, was finished, did she look at the Earl as if for instructions, and he said:

"Now I will take you home. We are perhaps 'going away' in a somewhat unconventional manner, but I feel you and I have a lot to talk about, Valencia."

She felt her heart give a frightened little leap in case she had done anything wrong, but he was smiling.

She kissed her father and he said:

"As you have always filled in the entries in the Register for me, perhaps it would be a good thing for you to do it today, so will you take it back to where it belongs in the Vestry."

It was true that because Valencia had such good hand-writing she had filled in the last three entries.

They were the Christening of two children born on the estate and the wedding of the estate carpenter to a girl from the village.

She, therefore, handed the Register to the Earl to carry as they went back along the covered way.

As he set it down on a table in the Vestry she saw there was a quill pen and a small pot of ink waiting for her.

"I suppose it was you who arranged with Papa that I should fill in the details in the Register?" Valencia said.

"I did not think your father would want to tell a

lie," the Earl explained. "I told him what had occurred last night, and he understood without my la-
bouring the point that Lady Hester would, if she
could, make trouble, which is something that must
be avoided at all costs."

Valencia was rather surprised that her father had
acquiesced so easily.

She knew he would think it wrong that they
should be married in such unusual circumstances.

She did not comment, however, but merely filled
in the Register.

She made the date of their marriage the last day
the Earl had been at the Priory before he returned to
London.

They left the book where it was always kept and
walked through the Chapel and out into the passage.

There the Earl stopped.

When Valencia, who was holding her train,
looked at him enquiringly, he said:

"I have tried to remember all the customs a bride
expects on her wedding-day, and as I am unable to
carry you over the threshold of my front-door, I shall
have to do it here."

Valencia gave a little laugh because what he said
was so unexpected.

Then he picked her up in his arms and carried her
up the stairs.

It made her heart beat frantically.

She was very conscious of how strong he was and
how easily he carried her.

Just for a moment she shut her eyes and thought
how perfect this would be if only he loved her as she
loved him.

Then she told herself once again that she should be grateful for small mercies and not be greedy and ask for too much.

She could not prevent herself, however, from putting her cheek against the Earl's shoulder.

She thought it was the most thrilling thing she had ever done.

He did not put her down when they reached the top of the stairs.

He carried her into the room that had been the personal Sitting-Room of all the Earls of Dolphinston.

Valencia knew it well, for it was where the old Earl had always sat until he was so ill that he had to be confined to his bed.

It contained some of the most exquisite pictures in the house.

The furniture was covered with *petit point,* which again had been the work of the Countess Anne.

The curtains were of deep rose velvet and were only a little faded with age.

But they were still as lovely as the painted ceiling, which was of cupids rioting around Venus being towed through the sea by dolphins.

The Earl carried her to the fireplace and set her down on the hearth-rug.

With his arms still around her shoulders, he said:

"It seems a strange sort of wedding, Valencia, and one you could never have expected, but I hope it will be one you will remember."

There was a note in his voice which made her ask:

"Is that why, rather daringly, you let me wear this beautiful tiara and veil?"

"I wanted you to feel married," he said, "and every bride wants to wear a veil. The only thing I forgot was a bouquet."

Valencia laughed as if she could not help it.

"You planned everything so cleverly," she said, "and now I know why you were so brilliant as a soldier."

"I have been fighting a very different sort of battle recently," he said, "but I cannot claim the spoils of victory, because they are yours."

He spoke as if he thought that everything was safely behind them, but Valencia asked nervously:

"You are quite . . . certain now that Lady Hester can no longer harm you?"

"Thanks entirely to you," the Earl replied, "she is defeated for all time. You are my wife and nothing and nobody can make her, as she intended, the Countess of Dolphinston, so we need think of her no more."

Valencia drew in her breath.

Then she moved away from the Earl to walk to the window and look out over the garden to the lake and the Park beyond it.

It was more beautiful at this time of the year than at any other.

The lilac and syringa were in bloom, and some daffodils still lingered under the trees.

The tulips made vivid patches of colour, as did the irises round the lake.

The wonder and loveliness of the Priory and its setting seemed to live in Valencia's heart.

Then she said in a strange little voice which the Earl had not heard before:

"I . . . I have something to . . . tell you."

"What is it?" he asked.

He had not moved from the fireplace, where she had left him.

He thought as the sun sparkled dazzlingly on her tiara, and with her veil falling over her shoulders, she seemed insubstantial and ethereal.

It was impossible that any woman could look more lovely.

"I was thinking while . . . you were driving . . . me here," Valencia said, "what I could do to . . . help you."

"Help me?" the Earl enquired. "You have done that already."

"Yes . . . I know . . . but we have . . . to think of the . . . future."

"And what of it?"

Valencia stood very still, looking out of the window with worried, unseeing eyes.

"I have thought of what we can do . . . when Lady Hester is . . . no longer a menace."

"I do not understand," the Earl replied.

"It is obvious now that she cannot marry . . . you that she will try to find somebody else so that she can . . . pay off her . . . brother's debts."

"You are right, she will certainly want some fool to take my place," the Earl agreed. "As she is so beautiful, there are doubtless a great number of men who would think it a privilege to be her husband."

There was a note of sarcasm in his voice which Valencia did not miss, and she said:

"Once she is . . . married . . . you will be . . . free of her . . . as you . . . wish to be."

The Earl did not speak, he merely looked at her and she went on:

"I . . . I therefore thought . . . you would be safe if I . . . then disappeared."

"How could you do that?" the Earl enquired.

"I . . . thought," Valencia faltered, "that . . . when you would wish to be free . . . Papa and I could go to . . . live in Greece . . . and we would not . . . trouble you . . . anymore."

She paused, then continued:

"You could say I had . . . left you . . . and if you wished . . . to marry again . . . you could announce that I was . . . dead . . . no one would . . . be any the . . . wiser."

The Earl did not speak and she thought he was thinking over the idea and she said quickly:

"Because you are so clever you could easily think out the details . . . but I am afraid . . . Papa and I would have to . . . ask you for a little . . . only a little money . . . as he would lose his . . . stipend if he were no . . . longer your . . . private Chaplain."

"I see you have thought it all out very cleverly," the Earl said after a pause, "but you have forgotten something which is very important."

Valencia turned round to look at him.

"What . . . have I . . . forgotten?" she asked.

"My wishes in the matter."

"B-but . . . I was thinking of you. I was thinking how . . . tiresome it must be . . . for you to be m-married when you . . . want to remain . . . single."

"And perhaps you had no wish to marry either."

Valencia's eyes flickered and she looked away from him.

"That is . . . immaterial."

"I think it is very important," the Earl contradicted her. "After all, when I arranged for my grandmother to present you as a debutante, it was obvious, being so beautiful, that there would be a number of men who would want you as a wife."

"I was not . . . interested in . . . them."

"Why not?"

The Earl's question sounded sharp.

She thought that the very easy answer to that was the one she could not give him.

"If you sent us . . . to Greece," she said evasively, "I should be . . . quite . . . happy to be with . . . Papa."

"Looking as you do, and being what you are," the Earl said quietly, "do you think it right that you should not be married and have a husband to look after you and, of course, a family of your own."

"I should be . . . all right."

"I do not believe that is true, and what I really want to know, Valencia, is why you should wish to leave me."

He looked at her questioningly and continued:

"I thought you wanted to help me and make certain I did the right thing by all the people you tell me are so important here at the Priory."

He paused before he continued:

"And, of course, on the other estates which I own but with which you have not yet concerned yourself."

"You are . . . a man and you know . . . what to do," Valencia said, "and you were . . . wonderful with the farmers . . . who were so happy to meet . . . you. You do not . . . need me . . . anymore."

"I think that is for me to say, and I find it rather strange, Valencia, that we should be having this conversation on our Wedding-Day!"

"Of course it is . . . strange," Valencia answered, "but so was our . . . wedding, with a bridegroom who did not . . . really want to be . . . married."

"You did not hear me say so today."

"No, but I am sure you are . . . thinking it. You did tell me you had no wish to marry . . . Lady Hester or . . . anybody else!"

There was a little sob on the last word which Valencia could not prevent.

Because she felt embarrassed, she turned once again to look out of the window.

"There is something I want to explain to you," the Earl said, "so come here."

Because the tears were pricking her eyes she did not move, and after a moment he said:

"Only a short time ago you promised to obey me and I have told you to come here!"

Quickly and surreptitiously she wiped the tears from her eyes.

Then she slowly moved towards him.

He waited until she had reached him.

As she looked up a little uncertainly into his face, she realised with surprise that she had never seen him look so happy.

"My darling, my absurd, ridiculous, adorable little wife!" he said. "Do you really think I would let you go away to Greece without me?"

"What . . . are you . . . saying?" Valencia asked.

Now there was a definite fear in her voice because she did not understand.

169

"I am saying, perhaps inadequately, that I love you! Without Lady Hester's interference I had every intention of telling you so, unless you had found somebody in London you loved more than me."

Valencia made a sound that was a cry of happiness and hid her face against his shoulder.

His arms went round her and he held her close as she whispered:

"How . . . did you know I . . . loved you?"

The Earl smiled.

"You are aware that we both have a very acute perception. I thought you loved me when you nursed me back to sanity after I was drugged, and I was quite sure of it when you so bravely saved me from being shot by Edward Ward."

"So that was how you . . . knew I . . . loved you!"

"Have you asked yourself how we could each be so sure of what the other was thinking if we were not already part of one another?"

He felt Valencia tremble against him.

Very gently he put his fingers under her chin and turned her face up to his.

"Now there is no hurry," he said. "We are not rushing away from danger, being frightened or threatened, and so I can tell you quite simply I love you, my darling!"

His lips came down on hers.

Valencia knew that this was what she had been longing for and praying for, and thought she would never find.

He loved her, he loved her as she loved him.

It was so perfect, so wonderful, she thought she would die from the sheer glory of it.

The Earl went on kissing her.

She felt as if they flew together up into the sky and the rays of the sun enveloped them.

Everything that was frightening and wrong was left behind.

Only when he raised his head did she say the words that had been pulsating in her heart for so long:

"I . . . love you! I love . . . you!"

"And I adore you!" he replied, and his voice was unsteady.

He looked down at her face, thinking that no woman could look more radiant.

Still in a voice that did not sound like his own, he said:

"How can you be so perfect in every way and I be lucky enough to have found you?"

"That is . . . what I . . . feel about . . . you," Valencia murmured.

The Earl gave a little laugh.

"We have so much to learn about each other, so much to do. So much has happened so quickly that it hardly seems credible, but I would not have had it any other way."

"You . . . do really . . . love me?" Valencia asked. "I was afraid when I . . . loved you I was not the . . . type of woman you . . . admire."

The Earl's arms held her so close that it was impossible to breathe.

"You are everything I ever wanted," he said, "and thought I should never find."

"But . . . you did not . . . wish to be . . . married."

"I have never had any wish to marry anyone except you," he said. "My father taught me that women were treacherous and untrustworthy, and that is what I found every woman to be until I met you, and knew how very, very different you were."

"How can you say such . . . wonderful things to me . . . ?" Valencia asked.

Now the tears were back in her eyes as she went on:

"You are so magnificent, so brilliant, and you have done so many things in your life. Suppose . . . after we have been married for a little while . . . you are bored and want to go back to the . . . exciting life you knew in India, or enjoy the . . . beautiful ladies we saw at Marlborough House."

The Earl laughed.

"I have had quite enough excitement and danger in the last weeks to last me a lifetime, and, as for 'lovely ladies,' you cannot be so ridiculous as to think there was anybody lovelier than you at Marlborough House."

She blushed as he continued:

"And I have no intention of allowing you to be spoilt by living in that artificial Social World. We are going to live here!"

Valencia gave a little cry of joy.

"Do you . . . really mean . . . that?"

"Will you be happy with me, my precious, at the Priory, without riotous parties?"

"I want to be . . . alone with . . . you, I want to . . . talk to you, to . . . love you, and to . . . have you love me . . . ."

"That is exactly what I intend to do," the Earl said.

He kissed her again, kissing her until she felt as if she gave him not only her heart but her soul and her body.

They were all his.

It was the love she had longed for but had never thought would be so wonderful.

Only when they were both breathless and the Earl's heart was beating frantically did he say:

"I think, my beautiful darling, we should now return the tiara and the veil to their place of safe-keeping."

He smiled and then continued:

"I intend to inform the household that the Photographer has finished and he is going to produce a photograph of you as you looked when we were married secretly, before we went to London."

"Will they believe . . . that?" Valencia asked.

"I will make sure they do," the Earl replied. "Just leave everything to me."

She put her cheek against his shoulder.

"That is . . . what I . . . want to do . . . now and for ever . . . !"

"It is what you will do," he said, "and I shall be a very demanding husband, and, incidentally, a very jealous one."

Valencia laughed.

"There will be no need for that. I was thinking when I was in London that I . . . never met a man who could . . . compare with . . . you in . . . any way."

He ran his fingers lightly down the side of her face.

"You are so ridiculously, absurdly lovely," he

said, "I shall always suspect that every man who looks at you wants to steal you from me."

Valencia thought how not so long ago she had thought despairingly that he would never look at her or see her as a woman.

"Please . . . go on thinking . . . that," she begged, "please . . . go on . . . loving me! I want to help you, protect . . . you and look . . . after you, but I also want you to . . . need me and love me . . . as you do now."

"Everything you have prayed for, my darling, will come true," the Earl said, "and I want you, I want you at this moment as I have never wanted anyone before."

He thought she did not understand and with a smile he added:

"What I am saying is that you excite me."

He pulled her close to him again and said:

"Because you are so young, so unspoilt and innocent, I will be very gentle, my darling, but I want you as my wife."

He kissed her and now his kiss was different.

She felt the passion which was like a fire burning against her lips.

It seemed to Valencia to ignite a little flame within her breast.

It was different from anything she had known before.

Then, as the Earl kissed her and went on kissing her, she felt the flame increase and become like the burning rays of the sun.

She was quivering against him and it was difficult to breathe.

"God, how I love you!" the Earl said.

Suddenly he picked her up in his arms.

"Where are we . . . going?" she asked.

He did not answer, and she realised as he carried her along the passage that he was taking her to his own room.

Her whole body was pulsating with the excitement he aroused in her.

She longed to be alone with him.

For no-one to interrupt what would be the most perfect, wonderful moment she had ever known in her whole life.

The Earl carried her into what had always been the bed-room of the Earls of Dolphinston since they had first lived at the Priory.

The afternoon sun was pouring in through the windows, filling the room with a golden haze.

The great carved four-poster with its red silk curtains and the Dolphin coat of arms emblazoned over the headboard seemed enchanted.

The Earl set Valencia down on her feet.

Then, locking the door, he took off the tiara and put it on a chest of drawers.

He removed her veil, and as he kissed her, she felt his fingers undoing the buttons at the back of her gown.

"Y-you are . . . making me . . . shy," she whispered.

"I adore your shyness, and I adore, too, the fact that no man has ever touched you but me. That is true, is it not?"

"Of course . . . it is . . . true!"

The colour that came and went in her cheeks and

the way her eyes flickered before his made the Earl cast one glance backwards into the past.

He knew now that his father had been wrong—some women were treacherous, some were untrustworthy, but Valencia was different.

She was everything a woman should be, utterly and completely desirable.

At the same time, he knew as if an angel's voice had told him so that she would never know any other man.

No man would ever mean anything to her because of her love for him.

For a moment he felt that he must kneel at her feet and worship her.

She was so different from all the women he had ever known and whom he had cast aside as being beneath his contempt.

They were unfaithful to the men who loved them and they broke the vows they had made at the altar.

Then, because he was human, his love moved within him with the force of a tidal wave.

He found himself kissing Valencia wildly, passionately, and demandingly.

Yet he knew she was not afraid, and that her love was as great as his own.

Once again he lifted her into his arms and carried her to the bed.

Then he joined her and felt her trembling against him. He thought it impossible for any man to be so happy.

He had found what he had thought impossible.

A woman who loved him so much that she was

prepared to sacrifice herself and her future because of her love.

"You are mine—mine!" he cried.

He felt Valencia moving closer and knew her lips were waiting for his.

He found himself strangely and inexplicably praying that he would never fail her.

He kissed her cheeks, her neck, until her body moved against his, and then her breasts.

His lips held her captive and he made her his.

As he did so, they were enveloped not only with the gold of the sun but the light which comes from God.

Pure and perfect, it is the Light of Love.

Barbara Cartland, the world's most famous romantic novelist, who is also an historian, playwright, lecturer, political speaker and television personality, has now written over 450 books and sold over 450 million books the world over.

She has also had many historical works published and has written four autobiographies as well as the biographies of her mother and that of her brother, Ronald Cartland, who was the first Member of Parliament to be killed in the last war. This book has a preface by Sir Winston Churchill and has just been republished with an introduction by Sir Arthur Bryant.

Love at the Helm, a novel written with the help and inspiration of the late Admiral of the Fleet, the Earl Mountbatten of Burma, is being sold for the Mountbatten Memorial Trust.

Miss Cartland in 1978 sang an Album of Love Songs with the Royal Philharmonic Orchestra.

In 1976 by writing twenty-one books, she broke

the world record and has continued for the following nine years with twenty-four, twenty, twenty-three, twenty-four, twenty-four, twenty-five, twenty-three, twenty-six, and twenty-two. She is in the *Guinness Book of Records* as the best-selling author in the world.

She is unique in that she was one and two in the Dalton List of Best Sellers, and one week had four books in the top twenty.

In private life Barbara Cartland, who is a Dame of the Order of St. John of Jerusalem, Chairman of the St. John Council in Hertfordshire and Deputy President of the St. John Ambulance Brigade, has also fought for better conditions and salaries for Midwives and Nurses.

Barbara Cartland is deeply interested in Vitamin Therapy and is President of the British National Association for Health. Her book *The Magic of Honey* has sold throughout the world and is translated into many languages. Her designs "Decorating with Love" are being sold all over the U.S.A., and the National Home Fashions League named her in 1981, "Woman of Achievement."

In 1984 she received at Kennedy Airport America's Bishop Wright Air Industry Award for her contribution to the development of aviation; in 1931 she and two R.A.F. Officers thought of, and carried, the first aeroplane-towed glider air-mail.

Barbara Cartland's Romances (a book of cartoons) has been published in Great Britain and the U.S.A., as well as a cookery book, *The Romance of Food,* and *Getting Older, Growing Younger*. She has recently written a children's pop-up picture book, entitled *Princess to the Rescue*.

More romance from
BARBARA CARTLAND

BARBARA CARTLAND

Called after her own
beloved Camfield Place,
each Camfield novel of love
by Barbara Cartland
is a thrilling, never-before published
love story by the greatest romance
writer of all time.